STEFAN'S STORY

VALERIE HOBBS

Stefan's Story

FRANCES FOSTER BOOKS
FARRAR, STRAUS AND GIROUX
NEW YORK

Acknowledgments: Stefan helped introduce me to the talented, wonderful women of my writing group: Judy, Lee, Marni, Ellen, Mary, Hope, and Lisa. They, and now Mary 2, have been my booster rockets and are dear friends every one.

Library of Congress Cataloging-in-Publication Data
Hobbs, Valerie.
    Stefan's story / Valerie Hobbs.— 1st ed.
       p. cm.
    Summary: Thirteen-year-old, wheelchair-bound Stefan renews his friendship with Carolina as they work together to save an old-growth forest from destruction by loggers.
    ISBN 0-374-37240-3
    [1. Friendship—Fiction. 2. People with disabilities—Fiction. 3. Forest conservation—Fiction. 4. Old growth forests—Fiction.] I. Title.

PZ7.H65237 St 2003
[Fic]—dc21   2002035314

For Diego

STEFAN'S STORY

October 13
Scattered clouds. Wind from the north at 5 mph
Time: 6:23 a.m.
Temperature: 68 F.
Barometer: 42
Waves: 2–3 feet
Sightings: Brown pelican, California gull, western
flycatcher, red-tailed hawk

～

STEFAN swept his binoculars slowly back and forth across his father's land. Nothing moved in the field, or in the shaggy eucalyptus trees along the cliff. The sky was clear and blue, wide and empty. Up in his "perch," as Stefan's mother called his room, he had the world all to himself, and he waited for something to wake up.

He waited and yawned and waited some more. And then his reward: a beautiful red-tailed hawk. The hawk glided in big loopy circles over the field as if it were no big deal whether it got its breakfast that morning. But Stefan knew better. The minute the hawk's supersharp eyes detected movement in the grass, it would dive faster than any human eyes could follow and be up off the ground with a mouse or a snake dangling from its beak.

Stefan wrote that down in his log: *Red-tailed hawk*. For the past five days he had seen the usual Pacific coast birds:

sparrows, gulls, pelicans, crows. But not the one crow he searched for like the missing piece to a puzzle. How would he recognize him? By now, Crow was a grownup bird, black and sleek and just like all the others. Unless Stefan found him, Carolina would never know for absolutely sure if she had done the right thing that day on the cliff when she made him fly.

Carolina. Did he really see her again? Was he dreaming?

If it *was* a dream, he could wake up, and things would be the same as they had always been between Carolina and him. They'd be kids again, and the best of friends. Better than the best of friends. They would know that no matter what, even if they were halfway around the world from each other, they'd be together in spirit.

Nobody could ever change that. Nobody but them.

But it wasn't a dream. He really had flown to Oregon, he really had seen Carolina, and things really had changed. Too much had happened in that short time to have everything be the same.

Stefan trained his binoculars on the tallest eucalyptus tree because it was the one birds liked best, and he searched its branches for Crow. It was not very scientific to let one single bird get to your heart, but he couldn't help it. He'd promised Carolina he'd watch for Crow forever, and that's what he would do.

Even when he knew that he was not likely to see him ever again.

1

D-DAY.

Stefan thought about a hundred ways things could go wrong or right (mostly wrong). Ways somebody could mess up (probably him) and ways the whole thing could collapse like a week-old birthday balloon.

They got ready in plenty of time to get to the airport. His mother was nervous and rang for Roberto to bring the car around three hours before Stefan's plane was scheduled to leave.

"Are you sure you have everything?" she said at least ten times.

"Relax, Madeleine," his father said. "Relax, dear." It was hard to know exactly what she was worried about. That Stefan wouldn't come back? That his plane would crash? Stefan told her the odds for planes going down, and the odds that he would stay forever with Carolina's family were double that:

about thirty-two million to one. But that didn't slow her down, not a bit.

She fussed around so much, checking the Weather Channel, opening and closing Stefan's suitcase, demanding to see his ticket, that by the time they finally hit the road, Roberto had to break the speed limit to get them to the airport on time.

Until he saw the huge silver jetliners waiting on the tarmac, it wasn't quite real to Stefan that he was finally going to fly in one. Families like his, families with what his father called "a relatively sizable fortune," had probably gone around the world half a dozen times. But the Crouches were the stay-at-home type. ("Crouch Potatoes," his father said, trying to be funny.) Stefan's father flew several times a month on business, so the rest of the time he wanted to stay home.

Stefan's mother was another story. She got claustrophobic on airplanes—she fainted on a vacation to Hawaii when Stefan was a baby and hadn't flown since—so that took care of any trips they might have taken by plane.

Thinking about flying for the first time (if you didn't count the baby trip) took Stefan's mind off the rest of it: After two long years, he was finally going to see Carolina again. He'd battled so long and so hard with his mother, it wasn't until she finally gave in that he stopped to think about what he had been asking for. Then he sort of panicked, but of course he couldn't back down. He'd already called Carolina and told her he was coming.

So all the way to the airport, then through the lobby to the ticket counter with a pit stop in between, he tried not to think about Carolina and thought about flying instead.

From the viewing window, the plane he was to board looked huge, a big silver tunnel more or less, closed at both ends, with wings that looked too clumsy and heavy to keep the thing in the air. But he wasn't disappointed. He knew that magic had a way of disappearing when you got too close.

His mother was behind him, but he didn't want her to be there, so he sort of didn't hear what she said the first time.

"Stefan, I'm talking to you." So then he had to turn and let her tell him for the second time that Father had gone to find an airline attendant, and that he'd be back as soon as he'd done that.

His chair made things so complicated. The airline couldn't just let him wheel himself onto the plane. Somebody had to go with him. It was because of insurance, they said. But of course his mother was relieved that someone would be watching over her baby. Stefan groaned.

"What, dear?" his mother said.

"Nothing, Mother." What good was it to be a teenager if your mother didn't know it yet?

"We packed your blue sweater, didn't we? The woolen pullover? You know the one I mean. The one Grandmother Crouch brought back from Scotland." His mother fidgeted with the little sausage roll of hair at the back of her neck.

Stefan said he was sure the sweater was packed, even though he wasn't. His mother had packed and repacked his suitcase a dozen times, putting sweaters and jackets in and taking them out again. The Weather Channel would tell her one thing one day and another thing the next. He'd never seen her so frustrated, but then he'd never seen her so worried either.

For his part, he didn't care much what she packed, not then. Not until later, when he remembered too late that Carolina was a teenager, too, and that teenage girls cared about clothes.

"It gets cold in Oregon, you know," his mother said, bending over him like a great blue heron. She twisted the braided gold band on her watch, turning it around and around her bony wrist, then back went her hand to the sausage roll. Teeny beads of sweat had popped out all over her long pointy nose.

"Call me the minute you get there," she said. "You *will*, Stefan, won't you?"

"Relax, Mother," he said, exactly the way his father said it, in his father's quiet patient voice. For once his didn't go up and down like a rusty clarinet.

"You will, won't you? First thing."

He said he would. But of course he wouldn't. The *first* thing he'd do was look for Carolina, who said she'd be waiting right inside the terminal.

First he'd find Carolina. And if he could pull that off without making a complete idiot of himself, well, then he'd think about finding a phone and calling his mother.

Two years. Two long years since the summer when Carolina and he first became friends. He and Carolina and Crow.

Stefan's father came hurrying back, his blue-and-red-striped tie gone crooked. "I finally found someone to take you on the plane, Stefan," he said. "They make the rules, then you can't find anybody to help you!"

A young black man in a blue jumpsuit came strolling up, pushing an airline wheelchair. Stefan's father transferred Stefan from one chair to the other.

"Please make sure this chair gets put on the plane," he told the attendant. "He will need it when the plane lands."

"Yes, sir," said the attendant.

"Oh, dear!" Stefan's mother cried.

They all turned to look at her.

"You're leaving!" Her hands flew up to her face, as if to hold it on.

"Say goodbye, Madeleine. We're blocking traffic." Stefan's father stuck out his hand for a shake, man to man. "Goodbye, son. Have a wonderful time. Give Carolina our love."

"Don't forget the wedding present for Carolina's mother!" His mother leaned over and planted a big wet one on Stefan's forehead. Then she smoothed his hair back and stared into his eyes long and hard like somebody on drugs. "*Call*, Stefan. The minute you—"

"Madeleine, that's enough," Stefan's father said, and hustled his mother away.

"All set?" the attendant said.

"You bet!" said Stefan.

The attendant pushed him up to the head of the line where the families with little kids waited. Not cool, definitely not cool. But he was going to fly, and that was all that mattered right then.

Stefan went down the ramp, into the belly of the beast. And then, just like that, he was on the plane and ready to go.

Free. He was free! For the first time in his entire life, Stefan was going someplace without his parents. He felt like throwing a punch in the air and yelling out loud. He would have done it, too, if the gorgeous flight attendant wasn't standing right next to his seat. He watched her give the safety demonstration, taking the card out of the seat pocket in front of him, even though nobody around him did. It earned him a smile. He tried not to think about floating in the Pacific with his seat cushion that was to be "used as a flotation device in case of a water landing."

The big engines began to wind. Underneath, something gave, and they began to move. Nobody but him seemed to be paying any attention at all. They were flipping through magazines, looking tired and bored. Not Stefan. His heart had sprouted wings and was already flying. He had to keep swallowing to hold it down. Clutching the armrests with his sweaty hands, he stared out the window at the ground that slipped past faster and faster until everything was one great gray-green blur.

And then the plane just lifted, easy as that. He was on his way to Oregon.

2

His drool woke him up. It was dribbling down his neck into the collar of his shirt.

How could he have fallen asleep? He'd been so *sure* he wouldn't miss one minute of his first-ever flight. But once the plane was in the air, that was it, pretty much.

What was he expecting anyway? *Star Wars?*

He had dreamed about Carolina, the way he sometimes did when he was really missing her. This time the dream was about the morning they let Crow go, made him fly for the first time. Only in the dream Crow kept coming back until finally Carolina said they would have to keep him after all. And that she was staying, too. Her mother—she called her by her first name, Melanie—had found a job, she said. They wouldn't have to live in the ratty old school bus anymore. It was a happily-ever-after kind of dream, the kind Stefan could make happen sometimes, though he didn't quite know how he did it.

And then he started thinking about Carolina, not the way he knew her before but the way she'd be when he got there. He knew it was dumb, but until that minute he hadn't thought about all the ways Carolina would be different. And suddenly it made no sense that she would want to have anything to do with him. She was being polite, that was all, inviting him up to visit her family because she had stayed with his.

Thirty thousand feet in the air, and Stefan was thinking straight for the first time. *Of course* Carolina didn't really want to see him! Why had she ever bothered spending time with a weirdo who scooted around in a wheelchair and collected owl turds?

Thirteen. She was *thirteen.* The thirteen-year-old girls in his class at Country Day, the private school his mother forced him to attend, spent 90 percent of their time looking in mirrors or giggling at boys. Thirteen-year-old girls were different from eleven-year-old girls. Really different. They got their periods and stuff. Breasts and stuff. Why hadn't he thought about that before?

And why hadn't he known until then that the friendship ring in his pocket was about the dumbest thing anybody ever thought of? Thirteen-year-old girls were *weird* about rings, any kind of rings, even a ring made to look like a dolphin, which was the perfect thing for Carolina. Everything *meant* something to thirteen-year-old girls, every look, every word a boy said.

So he wouldn't give her the ring, that settled it. He'd give her the little crow print, but he wouldn't give her the ring.

Maybe thirteen-year-old girls were silly, but thirteen-year-old boys could be *really* stupid!

Stefan sat back in his seat and closed his eyes, and he began to think about the magical eleventh summer when Carolina and he had first become friends. If he thought about it hard enough, maybe some of that magic would follow him to Oregon.

It had never been meant to happen. Carolina and he were about as different as two kids could be, at least on the outside. She was poor; he was heir to the relatively sizable fortune. She loved to explore; he got around in a wheelchair. She lived on a school bus with her mother and baby sister, Trinity, the family roaming from one place to another like Gypsies; he lived in a huge house overlooking the ocean, dreaming of the day when he could leave home and become a world-famous naturalist.

The first time he saw Carolina was through his binoculars. She looked like a wild creature, small and skinny, with a dark tan and skinned-up knees. Her hair was a mess, a rat's nest, like it hadn't been brushed in a week. What could she be doing on Father's land, he wondered. That was when he saw what was in the basket she held in her hands. It was a bird! A baby crow. He was so surprised he nearly dropped his binoculars.

And then he got angry. He had wanted that bird! It was *his* bird. Wasn't he a world-famous naturalist-in-training? He should have the crow to study. But later, when he met

Carolina, he could tell right away that Crow was where he should be. Crow and Carolina were joined in the strange way of wild things. They went everywhere together, Crow on Carolina's shoulder. If that bird knew what true freedom was, he didn't seem to mind not having it.

It wasn't like that for Stefan. Until Carolina became his friend, his house had been a prison and his mother his jailer.

Which wasn't exactly fair to his mother. After his sister Heather's fatal accident with her horse, Stefan knew his mother was terrified that she'd lose him, too. He wasn't strong, she said. He shouldn't take chances. But Stefan never really believed he was fragile. And neither did Carolina. He couldn't walk, that was true, but he could do practically everything else. He had exceptionally strong arms, for instance, and he never caught colds. And he was very stubborn, which was a kind of strength. Even his mother recognized that.

He and Carolina began going everywhere together, and everywhere they went, Crow went. One of their favorite places was the harbor, where Red's fishing boat was moored. Red was Trinity's father, but Stefan didn't think Carolina would have trusted him even if he had been her father, too. He kept disappearing, she said, and whenever he disappeared, her mother would take off after him.

The saddest day of Stefan's life (except for the day of his sister's funeral) was when Carolina told him she had to leave again. It was time to teach Crow to fly, she said. Stefan had been right all along. They would have to let him go.

They took Crow to the cliff at the edge of the estate

where all the world was open sky and deep blue sea. Stefan watched Carolina take Crow into both her hands and say goodbye to him. He could hardly believe it when she tossed him into the air. And he stopped breathing when Crow dropped like a stone out of sight. But then his wings caught air, and pumping hard, he gained the sky. In no time at all, he was a tiny black pin dot on the horizon.

Flying in this airplane was as close as Stefan would ever come to understanding how Crow felt that day. But he knew it wasn't the same. Wild creatures, if they were left alone, lived a kind of freedom no human could ever really know.

The captain came over the intercom, saying the plane would soon be landing. Panic closed over Stefan like a huge black bag. He wasn't ready. He wasn't ready to wheel himself back into Carolina's world, whatever that world was now. He wasn't ready to meet her new friends who would look at him, even if they were nice, with that look that said he was different.

What if Oregon wasn't a wheelchair-friendly state? There were ramps and wide doorways in California, at least in most places, but Oregon? He wasn't sure. There were laws in every state, right? But he wasn't positive. He should have checked it out on the Internet. At home he had Lupe and Roberto to help him do the things he couldn't manage by himself. Now he'd have no one.

His mother had been right. He wasn't ready.

But it was too late for second thoughts. Too late for any-thing. Something was wrong with the plane. It had stopped dead in the air and was sort of floating. He could still hear the engines, but they sounded far away and puny. Outside the plastic porthole and down through thousands of feet of air was Oregon. Or was it? How could he know for sure? All around him people slept or read, unconcerned. One little kid sent up a howl, and Stefan figured he knew what Stefan knew: The plane was going down. Then came a muffled thud, and he figured it out. The captain had let the wheels down and was waiting for instructions to land. They weren't going to crash after all.

Stefan's ears popped as the plane quickly lost altitude. Then two sharp bumps, and the huge jet was on the ground, racing across the runway to whatever would happen next.

3

"STEFAN!"

Raggedy jeans and a light blue sweatshirt, a swirl of long golden-brown hair. Taller, thinner, but Carolina all right, the *real* Carolina, raced toward Stefan across the airport lobby. Behind her came Melanie, all wild curls and flying skirts, Trinity in overalls toddling alongside.

It was Trinity who had changed the most. She had been only a baby when they left.

Stefan's eyes flew back to Carolina. Her hair was full of soft waves now, instead of the knots and kinks it used to have, and her green eyes had glints of gold, like mica, that he'd never noticed before.

She was pretty, really pretty. He guessed she always had been, but for some reason Stefan didn't feel so good about that.

"Hey, Stefan!" Carolina laughed, poking his shoulder, their old way of saying hello.

"Hey, yourself." He grinned and poked her back.

"I thought you were bringing the hot new chair." She meant the state-of-the-art TiLite X that Stefan's mother had bought to replace the one Stefan really liked: his grandfather's old-fashioned, do-it-yourself wheelchair with the cane back.

"Changed my mind," he said and shrugged.

"Good," she said at once. "I can push you around. Just like before."

Which was just what Stefan wanted. Things exactly the way they were before.

He and Carolina grinned happily and stupidly at each other until Melanie dived in and hugged the breath out of Stefan. Her fishing-lure earrings jangled against his neck. "We're so excited you're here, Stefan! Carolina hasn't slept in a week!"

Carolina groaned. She knelt down to tie a sneaker that was already tied, her face bright red. Then Trinity surprised everybody by climbing right up into Stefan's lap, just the way she used to. "Push Twinity!" she demanded, pointing her fat little finger like a field general.

And that was the way they got through the hard part.

Well, *that* hard part, thought Stefan. Which wasn't so hard after all.

≫

Stefan almost expected to see the old yellow school bus waiting outside the terminal, even though Carolina had told him that they weren't living in it anymore, not since Melanie got her waitress job at Big Dot's. Big Dot's was the café Carolina would take him to, first thing she said, so that he could meet everybody—well, almost everybody—in Haskells Bay.

First thing made Stefan think about phoning his mother, but he didn't see a telephone anywhere, so how could he call? Of course, all the phones were probably *inside* the terminal, where he hadn't thought to look.

"There's Hank," said Melanie. "We brought his pickup truck so we could fit everything in."

She meant the chair.

A big man with a thick orange-red beard came around the front of a beat-up green pickup truck. Carolina had told Stefan all about Melanie's fiancé, but Stefan was still surprised by the size of Henry (Hank) Macias. He was about the biggest, widest guy Stefan had ever seen outside of TV.

"Stefan," he boomed, shoving out a huge rough hand. "Name's Hank. How was the flight?" He frowned down at Stefan, blocking the sunlight, and Stefan figured he'd better come up with something quick.

"Uh, fine. Great," he gulped.

Hank smiled, and his face lit up like a jack-o'-lantern because of some missing teeth. "Okay I pick you up? Put you in the truck?" He looked a little embarrassed then, hanging his thumbs from the pockets of his jeans that rode beneath his belly and his faded blue plaid shirt.

Stefan said that would be fine, and Hank reached down and lifted Stefan out of the chair as if he weighed no more than a bird.

"You can sit up front with Hank," Melanie said. "The girls and I will climb in the back."

But Carolina caught the look on Stefan's face. "Stefan and I want to ride in the back, Mom."

Stefan didn't know what surprised him most, the fact that Carolina wasn't calling her mother Melanie anymore, or the fact that she could still read his mind. She knew he didn't like people having to do special things for him just because of his disability.

Melanie hesitated, a frown forming over worried eyes. "Are you sure that's all right?"

"Hell yes, it's all right," growled Hank, and plopped Stefan into the open bed of the truck. He figured out how to fold the chair without any help and stowed that in, too.

Carolina climbed in and sat down.

"I can't believe you're here!" she said, gathering up her hair and twisting it into a rubber band. "I keep looking at you and thinking it's been two whole years, you know?"

"Yup," Stefan said happily, thinking how nuts it was to be counting the freckles on her nose.

The truck started up with a gravelly roar and a plume of gray smoke. Then it coughed once and died.

"I can't believe your mother really let you come!"

"Yup," he said again, feeling like a full-fledged moron.

He figured Carolina could tell how nervous he was when she asked, "You know what I sometimes like to do?"

He said he didn't, because he really didn't.

"I like to lie down back here and watch the trees go by."

It was a kid thing to do, and he was glad she had thought of it. They'd done a lot of sky-gazing in the big field between her bus and his house.

The truck stayed running on the second try.

"Okay. Sure," Stefan said, as if it didn't matter one way or the other.

So they scooted down and lay next to each other, their arms touching, and watched the clouds sail by. And Stefan finally believed that he was in Oregon, and that he really was with Carolina again.

4

THE truck bumped to a stop. "We're here!" Carolina announced.

Stefan saw that they'd arrived at a small shingle house—an old ranger cabin, Carolina had said—with a green metal roof and a big rock chimney. There were trees all around and a long dirt path winding through them down to the main road.

Hank set up Stefan's chair and lifted him out. That was when Stefan saw the ramp leading to the front door. The wood was clean and new, so he could see it had recently been built.

Carolina gave Stefan a quick look, reading his mind again. "Hank made it," she said quickly, "but Trinity thinks it's for her." Hearing her name, Trinity ran up and down the ramp several times to show Stefan how it worked.

And that was how they got through the second hard part.

A tour of the house took no time at all. Stefan would be staying in her room, Carolina announced as they went down the narrow hallway. That way she'd get to sleep outside in the old bus and have it all to herself. "I didn't think I'd want to see that bus ever again once we got a real house," she said, "but it kind of grew on me after all."

Stefan was relieved. Carolina's tiny room wasn't frilly like his sister's with the white four-poster and pink velvet pillows. Stefan's mother was keeping Heather's room exactly as it was. Forever, he guessed. Carolina's room looked more like his own, except that it didn't have all the cages for mice and ferrets, and it smelled a whole lot better. Tacked to the wall over her narrow bed was a big poster of redwood trees. The photographer must have taken the picture lying down so that the trees looked even more immense than they were, towering up through shafts of sunlight into a clean blue sky.

When Carolina wrote to tell Stefan about Hank ("Melanie got a good one this time"), she didn't tell him right away what Hank did for a living. Stefan belonged to the Sierra Club, so he knew it wasn't easy for her to finally write and say that Hank was a lumberjack. "It's what people have to do up here to make a living," she said. "There isn't much work."

Stefan opened his suitcase and took out two packages. One was the wedding present, a small crystal bowl wrapped all in white. The other was the crow print still in its brown paper bag.

"Stefan! It's Crow! It really looks like him!" Carolina exclaimed when she'd slipped the little framed print from the bag. Her eyes were sad-happy, remembering. "Of course, all crows look the same, huh?"

"Whatever gave you that idea?" Stefan said stoutly. "I'd know Crow in a minute if I saw him, and so would you."

She looked doubtful. "But you haven't seen him, have you? Not once."

"Not yet," Stefan said. "You never know, he could come back with his own family. Return to his birthplace for, like, a vacation or something." He shrugged.

"I'm so happy you're here, Stefan," said Carolina, hugging herself.

"Me, too," he said, light-headed with relief. Nothing had changed after all, at least none of the important things. He felt so good inside, he hardly knew how to explain it to himself. It was like Christmas or spotting the rarest bird in the Western Hemisphere. Better, even better than that.

As they went from Carolina's room toward the kitchen, Carolina leaned down and whispered, "Melanie made you a cake." Her soft giggle tickled his ear. "Wait till you see it! You know how she cooks!"

They came into the kitchen just as Melanie set the cake on the table. "*Voilà!*" she cried.

Stefan was glad he knew it was a cake. It looked like the Leaning Tower of Pisa, only with mud dripping down the sides. "Chocolate, Stefan. Your favorite!" said Melanie proudly. "I'm so tickled about having a real oven that I'm a baking fool!"

"Wow!" he said, and then, "Wow, thanks!" because he could tell how much it meant to her that he liked it.

He couldn't look at Carolina. If he did, he knew they'd both crack up. But Stefan would have eaten anything to please Carolina's mother right then, even the terrible tofu casserole she used to make. He'd missed Melanie. She was the kind of person who gave her heart away and trusted you, whoever you were, even if it hurt her in the long run. She deserved a good life and a real house. This house was tiny—the whole thing could fit inside the Crouches' living room—but it was a lot better than an old school bus with no electric light, no heat, no sink.

"We're normal," Carolina had written Stefan in one of her letters. "We're just normal people now." It was about the best thing she could think to be.

Melanie cut Stefan a huge piece of cake and another for Carolina, then an even bigger one for Hank. Luckily, the cake tasted better than it looked. And they could swallow it down with big cold glasses of milk.

They sat around the table eating their cake and watching Trinity smear chocolate all over her face. "Thtefan?" she'd say every once in a while. But she never really wanted to ask him anything. He guessed she just liked the sound of his name, or was practicing her "S"s. She was about as cute as kids got, with Carolina's soft green eyes and her mother's kinky-curly hair.

Melanie asked about Stefan's parents. She and his mother had hit it off in a funny way two years ago when Carolina lived with them. That was when his mother told Melanie, an almost-stranger, about Heather's accident. His mother never talked about that day, not to anyone.

"How's your father doing on his diet?" Melanie asked.

"He's not," Stefan said, and they all laughed.

Hank didn't say anything, though he laughed along with everybody. To get Hank to talk, Stefan soon found out, you had to ask him a direct question. Then he'd screw his round face up as if it hurt him to think, and he'd take so long to answer that you forgot what you wanted to know.

He was a tree killer, but it was hard not to like him. Even later, when everything went crazy and nobody liked anybody very much.

❧

The sun was setting by the time Carolina and Stefan got away by themselves. They could see it through the trees as they set off down the narrow dirt path, the orange setting sun and the silvery sea. Down the driveway went Hank, heading home. They waved, and he waved back. Pine needles crunched under Carolina's sneakers and the wheels of Stefan's chair.

"Let's go to the dock," Carolina said, steering Stefan down through the trees. "Maybe Otto is on his boat." They bumped hard over an exposed tree root. "Whoops, sorry!"

"Are you still fishing with Otto?" Carolina's best letters had been about the days she spent with Otto Berne learning to fish for crabs.

Stefan heard the shrug in her voice. "When he lets me. He still thinks I'm a girl." She laughed, and so did he. "He says I can help him out until his grandson comes up from Los Angeles."

"Is he coming soon?"

"Any day now. Otto needs the help—he's getting old. Grouchy, too."

"Great!" Stefan teased. "A grouchy old fisherman. I can't wait."

But Carolina felt sorry for Otto. "He says when the loggers start taking the trees in Haskells Bay, the runoff will kill everything. Fish, shellfish, everything but the sharks."

They crossed the road, then hugged the strip between the asphalt and the trees until they came to a place where they could see the ocean again. The sun was almost gone, and the dock stretched out in dark silhouette against the fading orange light.

"I suppose he's not the only one, huh? Mad about that."

"Nope. It's fishermen against loggers, and fishermen's families against loggers' families. Everybody says they have a right to make a living. Everybody's got something to say!"

"Except the trees and the fish."

"Except the trees and the fish," she repeated. "And the spotted owls. But you know all about that."

That set up an alarm in Stefan. "They wouldn't cut down an *old-growth* forest, would they? I mean, who would do that?"

They had come to the first of a half-dozen fishing boats lined up along the dock. Carolina said that if you wanted a boat named after you, it helped to have a middle name. They passed the *Mary Louise*, the *Selma May*, and the *Juliet Rae*. When they got to the *Hannah Marie*, Carolina pushed the brake on Stefan's chair. He could see that what he'd said had set her thinking. "There's some talk that they're gonna do that," she said softly.

"Cut down the old trees? You're kidding!"

Carolina knew about the ecosystem of the old-growth forests, how everything depended on everything else to survive, from the lowliest centipede to the endangered spotted owl and marbled murrelet.

"Would *Hank* do that? I mean, if he knew about the owls and all?"

Carolina called Otto's name but didn't get an answer. "Well, I don't think he'd be happy about it," she said. Stefan could hear her need to defend Hank, who was going to be her stepfather in less than a week. She called Otto's name again, and this time a light popped on in the pilot's cabin.

"That you, girlie?"

"Yeah, it's me, Otto," she answered, laughing. "He calls me that to bug me," she told Stefan, then she called up, "I've brought somebody for you to meet."

A shadowy shape leaned over the rail. "I thought you was that scalawag I sent out to get me some eats."

"And some whiskey," said Carolina, just loud enough for Stefan to hear.

"What you say, girlie? Who ya got there anyway?" He had the breathless sandpapery voice of a longtime smoker.

"This is Stefan! Remember? You said he could go out with us tomorrow."

Otto leaned farther over the side, trying to make Stefan out in the gathering darkness. His cigarette winked once, bright. "What you got there, some kind of wheelchair?"

Carolina chuckled. "Some kind, yeah."

"You didn't tell me nothin' about no wheelchair, girlie."

"Guess I forgot," she said with a shrug.

"We can't take no wheelchair, Carolina."

"Sure we can, Otto. Stefan's been to sea before. It's okay."

"No way," he muttered, "*no way* I'm gonna take no . . ." The word he couldn't think of, or else couldn't say, floated in the air somewhere between them.

"Carolina?" Stefan said, nudging her arm, but he could feel her gathering up inside for a fight. He just wanted to get out of there.

"What do you mean, no way?" Fists on her hips, her chin lifted, she stared daggers through the darkness at Otto.

"Forget it, Carolina," Stefan said. "Come on, let's go."

"I mean no way, girlie. No way I'm taking him out there."

"Then you won't be taking me either!" she yelled. "Never again. Then what'll you do if your grandson doesn't show? Huh? What then?"

"Why didn't you tell him about the chair?" Stefan asked.

"Stupid old man," she muttered.

"What you say, girlie!"

"Carolina, why didn't you tell him?"

Carolina gave Stefan a blank look as if she didn't understand the question. Then she tilted her face toward Otto again. "You owe me for the last two times, Otto. Don't forget that."

"I ain't forgettin'."

"I'm just reminding you," she said. "Figure I have to, since you're not a man of your word."

Things got awfully quiet for a minute. As if there were other people, other things listening in. Then Otto said, "What do you mean by that, girlie?"

"You know what I mean, Otto. You promised to take me and my friend fishing. It was a promise, remember?"

Silence. Then: "Man of my word, huh?" The cigarette winked.

"That's what you told me," Carolina said.

They could hear Otto muttering, arguing with himself. "Well, all right, then," he said at last. "But if you cost me a day's work, you two, I'll have both your hides!"

"Forget it, Carolina," Stefan said again. "It doesn't matter that much."

"It does, Stefan," she said, turning her fire on him. "It does."

"First light," Otto growled. "Don't be late." His dark shape disappeared.

"All right!" cried Carolina, holding up her hand for a high five.

Stefan gave her hand a halfhearted slap. "You didn't tell him about the chair?"

Carolina shrugged. "I forgot."

"You forgot?"

"Yeah." She shrugged again. "It's not, like, the first thing I think about. It's not, like, you."

Stefan grinned so wide, he thought his face would crack. "So what did you tell him?"

"Well, what do you think? I told him you were going

to be a world-famous naturalist, what else? I told him you knew more about crabs and lobsters than he did!"

"You lied!"

"A little," she admitted.

She kicked the brake and turned the chair back in the direction they'd come. "Don't let Otto get to you," she said. "He's not as bad as he sounds. He's old, that's all. Things are changing too fast for him, and he doesn't know what to do about it."

There were no streetlights to guide them, and they hadn't thought to bring a flashlight, but Carolina knew the way home. It was strange for Stefan being pushed again, but nice, too. He was tired and closed his eyes for a little while, feeling the bumps of rocks and roots under Grandpa's skinny tires, and when he opened them again, the world had turned pitch-dark. They were going up the path through the trees, and the lights of Carolina's little house had not yet come into view. He felt goose bumps prickle his arms. It didn't make much sense to him then, but for some reason he was afraid. It was almost as if he sensed something ahead of them, looming in the dark. Something he couldn't yet see.

"Carolina?"

"Yeah?"

Like Trinity, he had said Carolina's name just to hear himself say it. "Nothing," he said.

They went around a huge Douglas fir. Then the lights of the house came up, illuminating the ridge and a stand of furry spruce at the end of the path.

"Stefan?"

"Yeah?"

"Nothing."

"No fair!"

"You did it first," she said.

5

HANK became Stefan's helper. He didn't make a big deal about it, he was just there when Stefan needed him to be. When Stefan asked Carolina why Hank wasn't out cutting down trees, she said he'd just finished a job up north and was waiting to start a new one. While he waited, he'd replaced the back door that had been falling off its hinges, unplugged the chimney, and built the ramp. Hank was one of those people who could figure out how to work with anything if he got a good look at it, even thirteen-year-old boys in wheelchairs who had to use a closet-sized bathroom and take a shower now and then.

Stefan's first morning in Oregon, crab-fishing day, Melanie made bologna sandwiches to take aboard the *Hannah Marie*. She put them in a grocery bag with a bottle of water and squished chocolate cake for dessert. Carolina put the bag in Stefan's lap, but as they headed out the door, Trinity burst into tears. "That's because of you, Stefan." Melanie laughed. "She never cries to go with her big sister. Do you, Trinity?"

Which only made Trinity howl louder.

"I'll bring you a surprise," Stefan promised. She gulped and started to hiccup.

"Yeah," said Carolina, wriggling her fingers. "An eel! How would you like a big slimy eel?"

Trinity nodded up and down, two fingers stuck in her mouth, her green eyes wide.

"Does she know what an eel is?" Stefan asked Carolina as they headed down the path. The sun was up, but the day was smudged over with thick gray clouds.

"Nope," she said, laughing.

❧

Carolina had said that Otto was old, she just hadn't said how old. He was stooped and white-headed, with a badly weathered red face and shaky hands.

Otto didn't do much fishing anymore, just enough to buy fuel for the boat and food for himself. And of course his whiskey and cigarettes. He let Carolina help out because she was strong and because she would work for whatever he could pay. It took more hands than he could put to work even in the best of times to man a crab and lobster boat.

Stefan found that out soon enough. When they'd buckled on their life jackets and Otto anchored Stefan's chair with some weights he found in a tangle of fishing nets, they rumbled away from the dock and out into the blue-black water. Once Otto got Stefan settled in, he seemed all right about having him on board. Stefan could understand Otto's worry, but he was far too excited to think about anything besides riding the deck of the old boat. Otto Berne could be as grouchy as he wanted. After all, he was the captain.

A seagull had hitchhiked with them all the way from shore, perched on the roof of the wheelhouse, its beak to the wind. Otto shooshed the big gray bird away with a wave of a trembling hand. "Rats with wings," he muttered.

It was a wintry-seeming day, and Stefan was glad his mother had packed the ugly blue woolen sweater from Grandmother Crouch. They knew how to keep warm in Scotland.

He'd called his mother finally, right after dinner. He told her about the flight, about the weather, about Melanie, Carolina, Trinity, and Hank. He told her where he'd be sleeping and how Hank had become his helper. He told her about the Leaning Tower of Pisa cake.

He didn't tell her they were going crab fishing. She'd have sent the National Guard to bring him back.

Watching Carolina ready the traps and coil the thick wet rope made him realize how dumb he'd been to worry that they wouldn't be the same friends as before. That she had become *Seventeen*'s typical teenage girl, dying to try the latest nail polish. Carolina's fingernails were chipped and broken, worse than his. And if she didn't look exactly like a cover girl in her fisherman's sweater and thick rubber jumper, she looked just fine to him.

The *Hannah Marie* chugged through two-foot swells

that slapped softly against her sides. Stefan sucked in a deep cold breath of sea air.

With his binoculars Stefan was the first to spot the red-and-yellow flags where Otto had set a line of ten wooden traps strung together like beads on a necklace—a "short line," he called it—between flags stuck into floating buoys.

The engine burbled to a stop at the first flag, and they rocked on the swells while Carolina and Otto got the winch ready to pull up the traps. It was hard work, emptying crab traps. The traps were heavy wire cages with a hole in the top for crustaceans to find their way in. Once they were inside, there was no getting out. Otto made the traps himself, which is what most of the crab fishers and lobstermen did.

While Otto cranked the winch, Carolina hauled the first and second traps over the low gunnel, using every bit of her weight, nearly falling as the traps hit and slid across the wet deck like rocks down a shallow stream.

It wasn't easy for Stefan to watch her work that hard without being able to help.

But he *could* help. "I can do that!" he yelled to Otto over the sounds of the wind and the creaking winch.

"What say?" Otto's white hair flew everywhere, clinging like stubborn bits of dandelion fluff. He held a gloved hand behind one ear.

"I can do that, sir!" Stefan yelled, pointing at the winch.

A look of disbelief came into Otto's watery blue eyes, but a glimmer of hope seemed to be there, too. If Stefan could manage the winch, Otto could help Carolina with the traps.

Stefan was surprised Otto let her do it by herself in the first place. She had the will all right, and she was strong, but she just didn't weigh enough.

Otto stalled the winch and set it. "All right, then. Give it a try." He moved Stefan's chair and set him and the weights under the winch handle and waited, his fists on the hips of his rubber oilers. Stefan could see that Otto wasn't ready to believe he could do it. But like most people, Otto didn't really know how a manual wheelchair could build up a pair of skinny arms. In no time Stefan was winching like a champ, while Otto and Carolina hauled over the rest of the traps.

Then the sorting began. Into a big rubber tub went the spider crabs and a couple of good-sized lobsters. Out the scuppers went the "garbage fish" and the eels—but not before Stefan grabbed a nice fat eel for Trinity.

"You're kidding, right?" said Carolina, but she found a pail and half-filled it with seawater. The eel played dead in the bottom, sulking.

They shared their lunch with Otto except for the bottled water, which he turned down in favor of what he liked better.

"That stuff's gonna kill you, Otto," Carolina warned as the old fisherman tipped the dark bottle to his lips. Strands of Carolina's hair had escaped the rubber band and blew around her head in a halo.

"Things come to an end one way or t'other," muttered Otto, and bit into his half of Carolina's bologna sandwich.

"Well, you don't have to help it along," she said.

Otto squinted his filmy, red-rimmed eyes. "You kids think you're so damned smart," he said. "Think you got the world all figured out, don'tcha?"

That was bait. Carolina didn't go for it, and neither did Stefan.

"You watch what happens when them loggers get the okay to cut down Haskells Forest." He scratched a wooden match with a fingernail, and a flame shot up. He held it to the tip of his cigarette and sucked the smoke through. "Then you see what happens around here."

Carolina gathered up the sandwich bags and paper napkins. "But that's private land," she said.

"All the better," scoffed Otto. "Man can do what he wants with his own land, given the right price."

Carolina looked at Stefan, her eyes wide, then back at Otto. "Is that what's going to happen, Otto? Did Mr. Haskell, whoever he is, sell his land?"

Otto shook his head.

"Otto?"

"Old man Haskell's been dead fifty years. He sold it long ago. To some big tycoon up in Tacoma."

"And so . . . ?"

Otto shrugged. "I only know what I hear over at Big Dot's. Somethin' to do with the stock market. Computer stock goes down, those big old trees start lookin' pretty good." Otto closed his eyes and laid his head back. Soon he was snoring, his big red nostrils flaring.

"What if it's true, Stefan?" Carolina looked the way

Stefan felt, worried and helpless. If they were going to start cutting down an old-growth forest, he sure as heck didn't want to be around to see it. It would be like going to a funeral.

Still, he didn't want Carolina to have to watch it happening without him there.

"Maybe we can do something," he said.

"What? What can we do?" She bit a thumbnail, as she did whenever she was worried.

"I don't know. Something!"

"Maybe it's a rumor," she said after a while.

"Maybe," he said.

Otto let out a bloodcurdling yell and woke himself up. "Damned cowboys!" he cried, for no reason they could figure, and got slowly to his feet, a hand bracing his lower back.

Since they'd finished sooner than expected, Otto headed the *Hannah Marie* north. He'd show Carolina and Stefan something they weren't likely to forget, he said.

They chugged along parallel to the shore. Seagulls flew in circles overhead awaiting their chance to scavenge the deck. Carolina sat on the wheelhouse, her long legs dangling, her boots nudging Stefan's shoulders.

The clouds had thinned, and the sun shone through them, dazzling the water. Always before, Stefan had figured he'd work in a college when he was grown, or a natural history museum, because what he knew best was mostly on land. But he'd begun to think that being a marine biologist might be more exciting. It would give him lots of time on the sea, where he was beginning to feel right at home. He wondered if Carolina was beginning to change her mind, too. She'd said she wanted to be a kindergarten teacher some-day, but that was before she learned to fish. Maybe she was thinking about making the ocean her life, too. And if so, she and Stefan could go to the same college, study together, and then—well, who could tell?

What was he thinking? He and Carolina had never talked about what would happen later, after they graduated from high school and went out into the world. What would she say if she could read his mind right now? He was thinking like— well, like a *girl!* Making silly plans, as if he and Carolina were boyfriend and girlfriend instead of just friends. If he didn't watch himself, he'd be writing her name on his note-book and drawing hearts around it.

It was being around her again that did it to him. When they were only writing letters, it had been different. You didn't get all stirred up writing letters. But he noticed things about Carolina in person that he'd never noticed before. Like the gold in her green eyes, which must have been there all along. Other things, too. She had short, stubby fingers, but they were strong-looking, and the thumbnail on her right hand was always chewed raw. She had hardly any earlobes—who but him would notice a thing like that? Maybe it was the rea-son she didn't wear earrings. And had she always had that tiny mole under her right eye? He didn't think so, but then he'd never looked at her the way he had been looking at her now. Studying her almost, the way he'd always studied birds and mice and snakes; the way he studied nature.

And then it hit him square between the eyes: It wasn't Carolina who had changed so much, it was he. Who but a nut like him would be happy just to have a girl's boots digging into his shoulders?

Otto set the boat to running itself and came out onto the deck. Carolina climbed down off the wheelhouse. "Watch now," Otto said. They came into a small cove, and Stefan's breath caught hard in his chest. Carolina clutched his arm. With disbelieving eyes they stared up at a huge section of land, a whole side of a mountain, that looked as if it had gone through a war. The trees had all been cleared away, all except for some sad stumps and branches scattered like arms that had surrendered in defeat.

"Clear-cutting," Otto said. "That's what you call that." He spit into the water. "Greed's another name for it."

Stefan looked up at Carolina, at the tears that glistened in her eyes, and felt like crying himself. Except that he was angry. He knew about clear-cutting, and he knew how stupid and unnecessary it was. If you had to cut down a forest, there were much better ways to do it. Selective logging was one. You didn't have to take all the trees, young and old, and leave the land bare.

"Look at the water," Otto said. They looked down then, thinking they'd see deep blue water. What they saw instead was a muddy red brown. "That's what kills the fish," he said. "Runoff. That and pulp from the stinkin' paper mills."

Otto stomped angrily back into the wheelhouse, and the *Hannah Marie* made a sudden turn, quick for her size. All at once the deck tipped, and Stefan flailed his arms for something to grab, but all he found was sky. In a flash Carolina lunged for his chair, grabbing a fistful of spokes. With every last bit of her strength, she hung on until the *Hannah Marie* settled down again.

Carolina and Stefan stared at each other, wide-eyed, each of them breathing hard. For a minute they couldn't believe what had nearly happened. "We almost lost Grandpa," Stefan said at last, trying to laugh the whole thing off.

"Stefan!" Carolina rasped in a choked-up voice, which to him said everything.

6

WEARY and fishy-smelling from their day at sea, Carolina and Stefan headed for Big Dot's, a trailer that had expanded itself into a friendly-looking café with bright yellow awnings and a wide front porch. They came to an abrupt stop at the steps. "Hank's going to have to build them a ramp," said Carolina, just as Hank came out the door.

"Need a lift?" he said, and Stefan was up on the porch and inside the café in two minutes.

Stefan was surprised at Big Dot. She wasn't big at all. She was shorter than Carolina, a shriveled-up lady wearing a greasy white apron, her gray bun stabbed with a pencil. She wiped her hand on the apron before sticking it out at Stefan. "Pleased t'meetcha," she said, all business, and turned back to the coffee she was making.

The room was filled with pictures: photographs of fishing boats, some of them wrecked and scattered in pieces on the beach; fishermen with their catch of various kinds; curling snapshots everywhere of Big Dot's customers looking well fed and happy. Over the windows hung stuffed fish coated with dust, a harpoon, nets with glass floats stuck inside, and, behind the cash register, a wheel from an old clipper ship.

The room was filled with men, too. Big men. Fishermen and loggers, Carolina said, though Stefan couldn't tell the difference between them. They all wore the same thing: plaid flannel shirts and worn-out jeans. They drank their coffee from the same big brown mugs. But Melanie said having the loggers there along with the fishermen gave the place the feeling of an armed camp.

Every last man turned to look at Stefan as Carolina wheeled him in.

They maneuvered past tables, through the room that had gone quiet, and up to a booth that Hank had saved for them. "Thtefan!" cried Trinity, which made Stefan smile. And then when Melanie brought a platter of fried shrimp with three different dipping sauces, Stefan forgot all about the loggers and the fishermen and dived right in.

Carolina was quiet, pulled inside herself. Stefan didn't know why, except that she was probably exhausted from yanking up the heavy traps. He was tired, too, especially his right arm. Trinity made up for Carolina's silence, babbling nonstop. She'd ask questions she already knew the answer to, then wouldn't listen to the answer. Stefan figured she'd have a lot of questions when she saw that eel.

Carolina was thinking about something. She kept staring

down at her hands and frowning. Finally she looked up at Hank. "Is it true that Haskells Forest might get cut down?" she blurted out.

It was a direct question, and Hank worked at answering it. "Well," he said. And that was all for a while. He stroked his beard and frowned. "Well," he said again.

Deep subject, Stefan nearly said.

"It could happen," Hank said. "I won't say that it couldn't. Word is, the land's been sold to Coastal Lumber."

"But that's who you work for!" cried Carolina.

"Yeah," said Hank with a short nod. His gray eyes were the kind with a thousand stories in them, good ones, sad ones.

"Well?" said Carolina. She'd gotten tougher in the two years since Stefan had last seen her. She wasn't afraid of sticking her nose into things, like a bear after honey, when she needed answers. He admired that.

"I gotta make a living, Carolina," Hank said quietly. "You know that."

"So you would! You'd do it! You'd actually cut down an old-growth forest?"

Hank said nothing more. He just looked at Carolina with eyes that said how much he hoped she'd understand, but of course she couldn't.

"Come on, Stefan!" Carolina said, sliding out of the booth. "Let's get out of here. I've lost my appetite." And she whipped Stefan out of Big Dot's faster than he could think about the lobster dinner he wasn't going to have.

And then they were stuck again. There was no way to get from Big Dot's porch to the parking lot.

"I can't believe it!" fumed Carolina. "I can't believe he'd actually work for somebody like that, some company that would cut down an old-growth forest!"

"Maybe he won't have to," Stefan offered.

"But just the fact that he would!" she said, pacing Big Dot's porch back and forth. Her jeans were torn. Salt crystals glittered in her hair. There was a purple bruise the size of a half dollar on her arm from where a crab trap had slammed into it.

"He doesn't think about the forest the way we do, Carolina," Stefan said. "For him it's food on the table."

"Don't you dare defend him!" she said, her arms crossed on her chest.

"I'm not defending him exactly," he said, defending himself instead.

"Stefan, you know how important this is. You of all people!"

They looked up as a big black Harley-Davidson skidded into the parking lot, sending gravel everywhere and dust into their faces. The rider, a tall thin boy wearing a black leather jacket and goggles, revved the engine several times, then shut it off. He stood for a minute with the bike between his long legs, looking up at the blue-and-yellow Big Dot's sign. His black leather boots had silver studs in them and came halfway up his dusty blue jeans to his knees. Slinging a leg over the saddle, he strode across the parking lot to the café.

Hank had come out, and a couple of his fellow loggers were behind him. One of them was his friend Dean, who wore an eye patch like a badge of honor where his left eye had once been. Logging was a dangerous business. He and Hank and the others came out the screen door laughing about something, kidding one another. Then they saw the boy in the black leather and stopped short.

The boy stopped, too, at the base of the steps. Stefan could tell by the way the boy stood there that he thought a lot of himself, or else was good at pretending. Ignoring Carolina and Stefan, the boy stared up at the loggers, his gloved hands on his skinny hips. Reaching up, he snatched off his goggles.

That was when Dean let out a big guffaw. "Why if it ain't a motorcycle-ridin' spotted owl!" he said, and then the other loggers—Hank, too—cracked up.

Carolina and Stefan could see why the men were laughing. The boy's face was covered with dirt, all except for two big white rings around his eyes. They watched those eyes grow dark and angry. He crossed the parking lot. Jumping on his bike, he kicked the starter and roared off down the road, showering gravel like BB pellets in his wake.

"Who *was* that masked man!" laughed Dean.

"Beats me," said Hank.

"I think he might be Zack, Otto's grandson," Carolina said quietly.

They all turned to her. "Otto says he lives in L.A." She shrugged. "He *looks* like he could live in L.A."

"He looks like he should go back where he came from," Dean grumbled.

Hank asked Stefan if he was ready to go home, then lifted him and the chair and took them down the steps.

Carolina wouldn't look at Hank. She just stepped behind the chair and got ready to push. "Too bad Grandpa can't shoot up a little gravel," Stefan said to get Carolina to laugh, which she did, but only a little.

7

ZACK and the big black Harley seemed to be everywhere that week. Everywhere but Big Dot's.

"He can't be helping Otto very much," said Carolina to Stefan. "We should ask him, don't you think?"

They had decided to do some research on old-growth forests and were on their way to the library.

"Zack?" Stefan asked. The farther they stayed from somebody like that, Stefan thought, the better.

"No, silly. Otto. We'll offer to go out with him again if Zack isn't helping."

Just then, as if he'd heard his name, Zack went sailing past on his bike. He wasn't wearing his goggles or a helmet. His shiny black hair blew back from a face as long and narrow as Stefan's, though nothing else about them was the least alike. Stefan's short, spiky hair was white. Not even blond, just white. And his eyes were the color of blueberry

Popsicles, or so Carolina had told him not long after they met. Before that Stefan had thought they were just spooky.

On his best days Stefan figured he was unique, what with the chair and all; on his worst days he was a geek, a dork, a freak. His father said those feelings were "par for the course" at Stefan's age. The people who loved him would forget all about the chair, the way his folks did, and Lupe and Roberto.

And Carolina, Stefan added.

His father tried too hard to make Stefan like every other kid in the world. Unlike his mother, who hovered over him, his father tried to ignore the chair and pretend that nothing was wrong, that his son had been born with working legs like most other people. Stefan should be happy he didn't have acne, his father said.

Well, neither did Zack. His face was smooth and golden brown, a built-in, born-on tan. Carolina and Stefan were about to go up the walkway to the Haskell Public Library, a wood-frame house with a picket fence and a flower garden, when Zack came roaring back. He was grinning. Why, they couldn't know. But when he smiled, he looked like a different person, a very good-looking different person.

"Hey!" he yelled over the rumble of his engine.

"Hi!" said Carolina. Stefan muttered something that passed for a greeting.

"Does this place really lock up at night or what!" Dark eyebrows were raised in disbelief over laughing brown eyes. He had the *Teen Magazine* heartthrob kind of face. A little too perfect, Stefan decided, and just a little too smug.

"The library?" said Carolina. "Well, sure it does."

"Ha! No!" Zack threw back his head as if Carolina had meant to make a joke. "The whole *town*. Haskells Bay. I mean, where do you guys go at night?"

"Go?" they said together.

"Yeah, you know, for fun." Zack cranked his handle grip, and the engine answered with a high-pitched scream.

Most nights, after reading to Trinity and putting her to bed, Carolina and Stefan watched TV or played Monopoly or Scrabble. It was just fine with Stefan, and it was what Carolina did all the time, so he knew it was fine with her.

"Well, during school there's some stuff," Carolina offered. "You know, dances. Sports."

Zack shot Stefan a look, taking in the old wheelchair and Stefan's thin legs. "Oh, yeah?"

Stefan was trying to think of a good exit line when Carolina said, "Your grandfather said you'd be going to school up here now."

"Don't tell me, let me guess." Zack put a finger to his temple like a cocked gun. "Haskell High. Am I right?"

Carolina laughed, a high and bubbly laugh that wasn't at all like her own.

"Haskells Bay General Store, Haskells Beach, Haskells Bay Bait and Tackle." Zack rolled his eyes and grinned at Carolina.

"Haskells Forest," Stefan said loudly, to remind Carolina why they were there, practically at the door of the library, and what they were there to do.

Zack ignored him. "Granddad says the whole town will

turn out for your mother's wedding this weekend. Maybe somebody will stay up past ten!"

Until then Stefan couldn't tell if he even knew who they were. But Otto must have filled him in.

Stefan was sure Zack wasn't helping his grandfather. He'd have had to change his fancy jeans for a rubber jumper. But what was *Carolina* thinking? That was what mattered. He decided to put Zack on the spot. "What do you think about crab fishing, Zack?"

Zack shot him a second look, this time a more careful one. "I don't, if I can help it." Then he winked at Carolina. Actually winked. Like a detective in a grade-B movie. Stefan couldn't believe it. And he couldn't wait for the motorcycle creep to leave so that Carolina and he could have a good crack-up. What a jerk the guy was!

"Well, don't do anything I wouldn't do," Zack said. Giving Carolina a little two-fingered salute, he roared off.

"Unreal!" Stefan said.

"Huh?"

"Can you believe that guy?"

"Huh?" Carolina was still gazing in the direction Otto's grandson had gone.

"I don't think he's going to be much help to his grandfather," Stefan said pointedly. "Do you?"

Her eyes came back from a long way off. Then she grinned like always, crinkling up the freckles on her nose. "All the better for us," she said. "We'll ask Otto if we can go out tomorrow. Want to?"

"You bet!" Stefan said, trying to ignore the exhaust fumes of Zack's Harley still lingering in the air.

≫

"Look at this," said Carolina, scrolling to an article in *Audubon*. "It says here that the marbled murrelet has been known to fly over forty miles from the ocean to return to the ancient forest where she nests. She isn't even a very good flier because she has such short wings. But she always comes back."

"So no forest, no marbled murrelet." Stefan sighed, downloading the article to print.

They had spent more than an hour on the Net scanning news articles and book reviews about anything having to do with forest preservation and logging interests. They found articles about protests, too. They learned that if you were willing to chain yourself to a tree or a bulldozer, you could shut things down for a while. But eventually they'd haul you off to jail if you were trespassing on somebody's private property. It was all too depressing.

"Did you hear about the Spotted Owl Helper?" Carolina asked Stefan.

"Is it some kind of parasite?"

"Nuh-uh," she said, and told Stefan about the guy who had brought a Tuna Helper box into Big Dot's with SPOTTED OWL pasted over the word TUNA and a picture of an owl on the front.

"Definitely not funny," said Stefan. "What did Big Dot do with it?"

"She threw it in the trash."

"Good for her."

"We've got to show these to Hank," said Carolina, stuffing the articles and the three books they'd found into her backpack. "Like this diagram that shows how everything depends on everything else to survive. Hank's like all the other loggers. He thinks you can just plant more trees to replace the ones you cut down and it's the same thing. I don't think he knows what happens in the old-growth forests. I don't think he'd cut them down if he thought a whole species could disappear!"

"Wait until after dinner," Stefan suggested.

"Why?"

"Mother says the way to a man's heart is through his stomach."

"That sounds like something your *father* would say."

"Maybe it was."

"Well, the way to a man's heart should be through his mind," she huffed, sliding her arms into her backpack. "A woman's, too, for that matter."

And with that high-minded thought, they left the library.

8

AT dawn they headed once more for the dock and the *Hannah Marie*. Otto had said the evening before that he'd be glad of their help, since Zack didn't seem too interested in much of anything but his bike. He was going back to L.A., Otto said, which pleased Stefan no end. Apparently Zack didn't like Haskells Bay much. "Hates loggers," Otto said, "for some reason."

Carolina had given Stefan a look that said she knew the reason all right.

"It's not my fault, girlie," Otto had protested. "First day the boy got here, he was all worked up over that logger—what's his name?—with the eye patch."

"Dean," they had both said at once.

"Yeah, that's the one. Like it was personal or something." Otto had shaken his head. "Well, the boy's got a temper."

Carolina had laughed then. "Yeah, like somebody else we know!"

~

In the morning Otto seemed surprised to see them, as if he'd forgotten all about the night before. But he quickly put out the makeshift ramp and, when Stefan and Carolina were aboard, pulled out a couple of big yellow rain slickers. There was a "sprightly little wind" out of the northeast, he said. No storms in the forecast, but "we wouldn't be gettin' no suntan neither." He tossed Stefan a floppy yellow hat. Stefan stuck it between his knees. If he absolutely had to wear the thing, he would, but not right then. Especially when, to Stefan's sorry surprise, out of the wheelhouse came Zack. He was wearing a pair of perfectly faded-out jeans and a white T-shirt that looked as if it had been ironed.

"Hey," he mumbled, in response to Carolina's greeting. She looked just as surprised as Stefan to see Zack on board. Hadn't Otto said his grandson wasn't going to help out?

With a grim look on his face, Zack grabbed his sleeping bag and took it inside.

"The boy's a little out of sorts," Otto chuckled. "Told him when he got in late last night that he was gonna have to earn his keep or go back to L.A. without a dime in his pocket." He shook his head. "His mother ain't sending him any money. She doesn't *have* any money!"

Zack came banging out onto the deck again. "Don't you have anything to put in this coffee? It tastes like battery acid!"

Ignoring his grandson, Otto went into the wheelhouse. The engine started with a deep rumble. Stefan decided to pretend that Zack wasn't around so that he could enjoy his day at sea. Why let a guy like Zack ruin it?

Carolina settled herself on the deck rail, her long legs and rubber boots stretched out before her. Balancing herself with the palms of her hands, she rode easily as the *Hannah Marie* barged through the choppy dark water. Stefan tilted his head back, letting the cold air hit his face like a zillion tiny gnats, and closed his eyes. When he opened them, Zack was beside Carolina. He was sitting in that same loose way, only he didn't look very confident. His knuckles were white, and he flinched when a spray of seawater hit his back. Stefan watched him lean over to say something into Carolina's ear, and he saw her turn with a puzzled look that said she couldn't hear him. The wind came straight at the *Hannah Marie*, whipping words away.

Zack said whatever it was again. This time Carolina laughed. Stefan tried not to wish that a good hard wave would send Zack flying, but it was no use. He hated the way Zack looked at Carolina, really looking now, not just skimming his eyes over the surface. What right did he have to look at her that way? And why didn't she just give him a good hard shove? Couldn't she see what kind of a guy he was?

Otto cut the engine when they got to the flags, which ripped and snapped in the wind. The deck pitched, as the *Hannah Marie* rode the big rolling swells like the old tub she was. Otto fed out the chain to set the anchor. At his order Stefan began turning the winch. Otto and Zack got to work, staggering and knocking into each other as the heavy traps came over the side. It was hard work, and Stefan was glad Carolina didn't have to do it, even if it was Zack who took her place. Her job was to stack the traps as best she could against the side. Once she slid all the way across the deck on her bottom. But she got right up again, grabbing a trap as it sailed her way.

Dark, ominous-looking clouds were building on the horizon. A thought crossed Stefan's mind that an old fisherman with as much experience as Otto might just guess at the weather instead of listening to the reports. Because somebody had gotten it wrong. As the last trap came over the side, it started to rain. Only a few drops at first but a promise of more to come. Otto went into the wheelhouse to start the engine. "Let's get inside," Carolina said. "It looks like it's really going to hit!" She glanced from Stefan to Zack, and Stefan could see she was going to ask for Zack's help to get him and the chair inside.

And he just couldn't do it. Couldn't let her ask. He saw himself rocking like a helpless baby between Carolina and Zack as they maneuvered Grandpa into the wheelhouse, and it was more than he could bear. "Go ahead," he said tight-lipped. "I'm staying out here."

Without a second thought, Zack ducked into the wheelhouse.

"Stefan! You can't stay out here. You'll get soaked! It isn't safe." Carolina had gathered her slicker up around her ears. Her hair was already soaked with sea spray.

Stefan pulled the floppy yellow hat from between his chattering knees and jammed it on his head. "I'll be fine," he said.

"Hang on, I'll get Zack." Carolina reached for the door.

"Don't you dare!" Stefan yelled. "Don't you dare tell me what I can and cannot do!" Something was slipping away. Stefan could feel it, and it scared him. It all had to do with Zack, with the difference between Zack and him. But he was too worked up to know it then, or to do anything about it. So he did the first stupid thing he could think of: He took it out on Carolina. "Leave me alone," he said bitterly.

Carolina stared hard at Stefan, and he saw her chin go up, just enough to let him know he'd hurt her feelings. Never before had there been a bad word between them. Stefan wanted so much then to pull his ugly words back from the cold wind they'd disappeared into, but he couldn't. He would not be weaker than Zack. He would not.

"Okay, have it your way," she said, her lips in a tight line. The wheelhouse door slammed behind her.

He knew he'd done it then. No way could he get out of what he'd gotten himself into and still save his pride. He could hear his father now: *Pride goeth before a fall,* he would say. But Stefan figured he could weather out a storm all right, the mood he was in. He'd hang on to the winch with his teeth if he had to.

Then as the *Hannah Marie* made for shore through five- and six-foot breaking swells, the real rain hit.

That's when Stefan, a southern California kid, learned the meaning of cold. His teeth chattered, even his ribs chattered, as the rain came down as if it had a problem with him personally. It beat like golf balls on his head and against his back as he bent forward, hanging on to the winch for dear life. Freezing-cold water found its way everywhere, around the collar of the slicker and down his back, into his ears and underwear.

Was he crying? He might have been. Wet as he was, it was hard for him to tell. As the *Hannah Marie* banged into the swells, and her deck vibrated under Grandpa's chair as if the ocean wanted to shake them loose and send them flying, all he knew for sure was that he had never been so scared or miserable in his entire life.

Twice Carolina's frightened face popped out the door. She yelled something each time, but the wind snatched it. With his free hand he waved her away. By then it was too late, and everybody knew it. If they had tried to get him inside, as wet and slick as the decks were now, they'd all have gone overboard.

So he hung on like an abalone to a rock and repeated every prayer he'd ever known, all except for the one that said, "If I should die before I wake . . ." It had scared him as a little boy, and it scared him a whole lot right now.

What was he trying to prove? And was it worth risking his life? Some things in life were, he knew that. The heroes in some of his favorite books, and in real life, too, risked their lives for what they believed in. That's why they were called heroes. But he wasn't anybody's hero, not here, not now, hanging on to the winch of a crab fishing boat in the middle of a storm just so he wouldn't be laughed at. He was just a jerk. No bigger or better or braver than Zack.

There were times when you had to do the braver thing, the thing that made a difference. But this, Stefan knew, as his arms threatened to give out, this wasn't one of them.

Just when he thought he could hold out no longer, when his life would become a second tragic story for his mother, Stefan felt the engine cut to an idle. The deck leveled out. Lifting his head, Stefan saw that they had gone into the bay. The sea was rocking the *Hannah Marie* as tenderly as a mother rocks a cradle. Overhead a flock of gulls, cawing, escorted the boat into the harbor. The rain had stopped, or, like a bad dream, they had left it behind.

9

STEFAN'S father was right. About pride, at least.

Peeling out of his soaked clothes that night, Stefan heard Carolina in the kitchen telling Melanie that if the storm passed over, they'd be going out again the next morning. Carolina had forgiven Stefan for being such an idiot, though he had yet to forgive himself, and by ten, as they sipped hot chocolate and read each other passages from their library books, the sky was clear and black. Stars danced, or seemed to, but by then Stefan was already getting sick.

He awoke the next morning with hammers banging in his head and a miserable sore throat. "Croak!" he said as Hank lifted him into his chair. Hank gave Stefan a funny look. "Hi," Stefan whispered, because that was about all he could do.

Hank wheeled Stefan into the kitchen. "Stefan's lost his voice," he said to Melanie, who took one look at Stefan and plastered her hand to his forehead.

"He's burning up!" she cried. "You're burning up, Stefan!" she repeated straight into his face, as if he'd lost his hearing as well.

Carolina came in from the school bus, dressed for a day at sea.

"Stefan's sick," Melanie said. "He's not going anywhere."

"Wait!" Stefan protested. "Wait!" But nobody was paying any attention to him.

"Oh, no! Stefan!" Carolina cried, kneeling at the level of Grandpa's wheels. "It's all my fault. I should never have let you stay out in the storm!"

"You did what?" said Melanie, wide-eyed.

Stefan tried to tell them both that it wasn't Carolina's fault. He tried to say that he *could* go fishing, that he wasn't *really* sick. Mostly he tried to insist that Carolina couldn't go without him. With Zack, in other words. But it hurt to talk, and nobody was listening to him anyway.

He watched miserably as Carolina laid out six slices of bread. Was she fixing a sandwich for Zack? They'd made a lunch for Otto the day before, which Zack ate. Of *course* she was making a sandwich for Zack. What a crazy thing, he thought: If Carolina weren't so thoughtful, he wouldn't like her half as much. He just didn't want those thoughts going Zack's way. Zack probably wouldn't even thank her.

Once she was gone, he felt a hundred times worse. Melanie fed him two aspirins and sent him back to bed. "I'll take Trinity to the park," she said, "so you can get some

sleep. Hank will be right outside, in the back clearing brush."
She gave him that certain look, a squint and frown that said
she was worried and that he'd better do what she said. He
was under mother-power now. "If you're not better by this
afternoon, we'll give the doctor a call."

"You knock on the window if you need anything at all,"
Hank said, setting Stefan carefully onto Carolina's narrow
bed with his tree-trunk arms. Dizzy, Stefan dropped into a
well of sleep, waking only after weird dreams, the weirdest
he'd ever had. In one dream a huge greenish-black mouth
threatened to swallow him whole. But instead of running
away from it, like an idiot he ran straight up its wet furry
tongue.

~

Something cool and soothing woke him. Carolina was sitting
on the edge of the bed. She had laid a wet washcloth on his
forehead. On her face was the world's saddest look.

"Am I dying?" Stefan whispered.

"Don't try to talk," she said. "I can't understand you
anyway."

But Stefan felt fine then. He wanted to get up. He needed
to ask her all about the day, the one whole day he'd missed.
He needed to know about Zack, about Zack and Carolina.
What he said, and what she said. What he did, and what she
did. He had to know *everything*. He raised himself on his elbows and tried to look recovered.

"You want to get up?"

He nodded.

Carolina brought Hank, and they all went into the kitchen. It was Melanie's night off, and she'd made chicken soup. Stefan knew what it was because there were actual chicken feet sticking out of the pot.

"Looks like it was only a twenty-four-hour bug." Melanie smiled, ladling soup into bowls and setting them on the small table. "But you won't be going fishing, Stefan. At least not until you get your voice back."

"Yeah," said Carolina, laughing. "What if you went overboard and couldn't yell for help?"

Stefan knew Melanie wouldn't change her mind, especially after his mother called and learned he had "a case of the sniffles." Stefan was grateful to Melanie for running interference for him. "It's not easy for her, Stefan," was all she said.

"Otto needs me tomorrow," Carolina announced, and Stefan's heart did a nosedive, "but I'll stay here with you, Stefan." His heart was the bobber on a fishing line. She could sink it with a frown, but if she smiled, up it went again. "Oh! I forgot! There's going to be a town meeting on Wednesday night."

"I knew there was something I was going to tell you," said Melanie. "The sign went up yesterday. I heard that somebody from your company is going to speak, Hank."

Hank screwed up his face. Was that a real question? "Farnsworth," he said.

"Farnsworth? That's a fancy name!"

"Owner," said Hank. "Owns the company." He frowned into his soup.

⤳

After dinner, when they were in the kitchen alone, Carolina told Stefan about her day without his having to ask. All the things he wanted to know, and some he didn't. Zack was in a band called the Snake Handlers in L.A., but he'd hocked his guitar to get the bike. His guitar had belonged to Jimi Hendrix, or so he said, and his bike had been Marlon Brando's, but Stefan could tell that Carolina had her doubts. She had given Stefan a pad and pencil to save his voice, but he didn't have much to say. Not about Zack anyway.

The weather had been perfect, she told him. The sea was calm, and several other crab boats had gone out. When the *Hannah Marie* reached the trap line, Otto manned the winch, while Carolina and Zack began pulling traps. "Where's my winch man?" Otto asked, and Carolina told him that Stefan was very, very sick. It was all Otto's fault, she said, even though she blamed herself. As captain of the *Hannah Marie*, he was responsible for all hands on board.

"So he took a slug of whiskey, right?" Stefan wrote, and drew a bottle with two "X"s on it.

"Right!" wrote Carolina. "What am I doing?" She laughed, handing Stefan the pencil. "*I* can talk!" She smelled salty and fishy and, to Stefan, better than perfume, better than hot apple pie, which was about as good as smells got. He knew he was grinning like a moron, but he couldn't help it. He was just so glad she was back where she belonged, here in this little cabin, with him.

"I made Otto take us north again so that Zack could see the clear-cutting," she said. "The more people on our side the better, right?"

Stefan didn't think Zack could be on anybody's side but his own, but he didn't write that. It was really only a feeling he had about Zack. He didn't have any hard evidence. So he nodded and shrugged and left it to her to figure out.

The more Carolina talked about Zack, the less Stefan liked himself. Always before he'd tried to be fair, to give people what his father called a "fair shake." And now he wasn't even trying.

"Zack knows all about protests," she said. "He was actually in the Los Angeles riots." She looked far more impressed than Stefan thought she should be.

"That wasn't a protest," he wrote. "It was a riot."

"Oh, well, I know." She frowned. "But he's had some experience . . ." Her voice trailed off, as if she really didn't know what she was thinking.

"Can he make a Molotov cocktail?" he wrote.

"Stefan! That's not funny. We could burn down the forest."

He rolled his eyes to let her know he was only kidding, which she should have known.

"A friend of his put sugar in all the police cars' gas tanks," she said. "I told him how dumb I thought *that* was."

"Nonviolent protest." Stefan underlined *nonviolent*. "Remember Gandhi," he wrote.

"And Martin Luther King," she said.

"And Tweety Bird," he wrote. The canary he drew looked more like a sick chicken.

"Tweety Bird?" Carolina giggled. "What did he do?"

"I don't know," Stefan wrote, "but he didn't get eaten."

Carolina cracked up. Then all at once she got serious. In the light that hung over the table, her green eyes sparkled gold. "Oh, Stefan," she sighed. "Wouldn't it be great if you lived here all the time? If we lived in the same town again?"

He grinned and nodded, his worries packing up and leaving all at once, like bad renters. He should have known Carolina felt the same way he did. He never should have doubted that.

"We like all the same things," she said. "We care about the same things! It isn't fair that we live so far away from each other."

"I totally agree," he wrote, underlining every word twice.

He was feeling better by the minute.

Carolina got up to make hot chocolate.

"Anyway," she said, stirring chocolate syrup into a pan of milk, "I explained to Zack all about the old-growth forests, and he agrees they shouldn't be cut down. So chalk one up for our side."

Zack again. The guy wouldn't go away.

"The town meeting is going to be interesting," Carolina said. "We'll hear what everybody's thinking. That way, if we decide to have a protest, we'll know how many people we can count on."

"*If?*" Stefan said, his voice cracking and hoarse.

"Well"—Carolina bit her lip—"if the guy from Coastal Lumber finds out that the whole town is against cutting down Haskells, well"—she put two mugs of hot chocolate on the table—"then maybe the company will go somewhere else!"

Stefan wrote, "Would Sylvester eat Tweety Bird if he could?"

Carolina giggled. "Maybe he'd ask permission?"

"Ha!" Stefan croaked.

"We need to go there, Stefan," Carolina said suddenly, as if a light had gone on over her head.

"Where?"

"Haskells Forest! Here we are talking about saving something we haven't even seen."

Stefan was surprised that she'd never been there.

"It's funny, isn't it? But we've only driven past it. Lots of times. It's right up the road. Two miles at the most." She blew on her hot chocolate. "I'll ask Hank if he'll take us there."

"Are you sure you want to ask Hank?" Stefan wrote.

"You bet! When he sees how beautiful the forest is inside, he won't want to cut it down."

"They're really sort of a mess," he wrote.

"Huh?"

"Old-growth forests." He wanted to tell her all that he knew, but he'd have had to write a whole essay or wait until he got his voice back. He didn't want her to have the wrong idea. In an old-growth forest nobody cleared away the dead wood. There weren't any neat little paths for sight-seeing. No bridges or signs or nice little rock borders. The whole thing just broke down and rotted, the way it was supposed to. Anyway, that was what he had read. Like Carolina, Stefan had never seen an old-growth forest up close.

"Well, we have to go there," Carolina declared. "Here's to Haskells." And they clinked their mugs together.

≈

Melanie said it wasn't fair to ask Hank to take them to Haskells. "You've hardly said a word to him lately," she reminded Carolina. "How do you think that makes him feel? *He* doesn't own Coastal Lumber."

Melanie said she'd take them herself. "I suppose we all should know first-hand what it is we're arguing about," she said. But they wouldn't be able to stay long. "I have to finish our dresses for the wedding," she said. "And you, Miss Lewis, need to stand still for ten minutes at a time so I can pin up the hem on yours. It's finished except for that."

Carolina made a face. She was a jeans person all the way. "Okay," she said. "If you'll take us to Haskells, I'll stand still for ten minutes."

"Deal," said Melanie. "After all, it's not every day your mother gets married."

"That sounds funny," said Carolina.

"Well," said Melanie, "maybe it does. But it's true just the same. It's going to be a beautiful dress, sweetheart." She gave Carolina a one-armed squeeze. "If there's one thing your mother can do, it's sew!"

Carolina looked at her mother doubtfully. "You've never made anything before."

"Sure I have!"

"When?"

"Oh," Melanie said, with a dismissive wave of her hand, "home ec. Years ago."

"Yeah, about a hundred!" smirked Carolina.

Hands on her hips, Melanie stared Carolina down. "Hey, smarty, you want to go to Haskells or don't you?"

"Yes! Yes! Please, O Great Mother!" Carolina fell to her knees and wrung her hands together.

"Give me a break." Melanie laughed and rolled her eyes.

⌁

Hank was quiet as he helped Stefan into the back of the pickup, but then he usually was. As they left, he slapped the tailgate the way cowboys slap a horse's rump to send it off, then turned back toward the house. There was a little stoop in his broad shoulders, but Stefan thought he could have imagined that.

Carolina and Stefan settled themselves against the back of the cab. The day was sunny and warm, and they closed their eyes, tipping their faces to the sun. The truck bumped along beneath them in a way that Stefan had quickly grown used to, a friendly sort of way. The way he'd gotten used to being with Carolina again, as if they'd never been apart.

But the way he felt about her was more than just friendly. He knew that now. He didn't even especially want it to be anything more, but it was. Since the first day on the *Hannah Marie*, he'd known. Maybe even before that. Maybe the minute he saw her running toward him across the airport lobby. Could he tell her? A knot of fear clutched his stomach. He *couldn't* tell her. It would be stupid to tell her, suicidal! But how else could he know if she felt the same way?

The warmth of the sun was suddenly gone, and he opened his eyes. They had entered a tunnel, a living tunnel. High above their heads branches of immense trees joined to knit together the rip the road had made. Not a speck of sky was visible.

Melanie pulled to the side of the road and turned off the engine. A strange kind of quiet happened then, as if they'd been touched with a magician's wand and were now enchanted. No one moved, not even Trinity. They hardly breathed.

Then came the call of a single bird, a towhee, Stefan guessed, and then another—an answer—from a different place in the forest. There were other sounds, too, but he couldn't identify them.

He scooted to the edge of the tailgate, where Carolina had set up his chair. She and Melanie helped him slide down into it. He gazed up at the trees. They had been there all his life and long, long before that, almost as if they were waiting for something. He told himself how silly it was to think that trees had human thoughts and human feelings. Trees didn't wait, they *were*. Just because it felt as if they were taking a breath and letting it out when Stefan did, didn't make it true.

Trinity had missed her nap and was now conked out in her car seat. "Let's try to get her into the backpack without waking her up," Melanie whispered. "She can see the forest another time."

"I certainly hope she can," said Carolina emphatically, her lips in a narrow line.

They searched for an opening in the trees. Back and forth they went along the road, but they could find no way through the green wall. When they were about to give up and look farther on down the road, it magically appeared: a narrow path in a place they'd already looked several times, as if it had made itself just for them, exactly a wheelchair wide.

Carolina didn't push Grandpa very far into the trees before she stopped. "Oh, Stefan!" she whispered, as if they were inside a church, under a cathedral ceiling that went up and up almost out of sight.

Covered with bright green moss, the ancient trees rose on all sides, looming over the visitors, their branches intertwined. The sunlight leaking through in long thin shafts looked smoky and dreamlike.

"Listen," Stefan whispered. They listened to the forest sounds, the steady drip-drip from leaves that had gathered the morning's moist air, a nearly silent clicking and snapping of life inside the stumps and the fallen trunks of the dead ones preparing their return to the earth, where long ago they'd sprouted as the tiniest of saplings. Birds called to each other about the strange intruders (one wore wheels!), and they could almost feel the eyes of rodents and salamanders, maybe even a possum or a fox, watching in the tangled undergrowth.

It was a mess, but such a beautiful mess. It made Stefan want to close his eyes and capture it on his eyelids so that whenever he wanted to have it back, he could. But he was beginning to understand, gazing up with Carolina at his side as if they were the forest's very first explorers, that life didn't work that way.

"It's the most beautiful place I've ever been," said Carolina. And then: "Where's Mom?"

They turned and saw Melanie behind them. With Trinity asleep against her back, Melanie was standing with her arms crossed over her belly—except that she didn't have much of a belly. She was weeping, very quietly, looking up at the trees, silvery tears sliding down her face.

"Mom?"

Melanie looked at Carolina with a faraway look in her eyes. "I didn't know," she said softly. "I didn't know it would be like this. They can't cut this down. It would be like—like killing people!"

"We'll stop them," Stefan vowed. "We have to!"

"Oh, Stefan," Carolina cried, "what if we can't? What if there's nothing we can do!"

"We'll think of something," he said, sounding surer of himself than he was.

"*You* will, Stefan," she said. "I know you. You'll think of something."

And from that moment some part of his mind was trying for all it worth to do just that. If Carolina believed that much in him, then he had to believe, too.

They drove back to the house without saying a word, all except for Trinity, who had awakened and was singing the "Itsy Bitsy Spider" song over and over at the top of her lungs. She already had her own little way of appreciating nature.

10

HANK was in the doghouse, as Stefan's father would have said. Carolina wasn't talking to him, and even Melanie had grown quieter when he was around.

Stefan was stuck somewhere in the middle. If he spoke to Hank, then he was being a traitor to Carolina—and to the trees in Haskells Forest, she would have said. But if he didn't talk to Hank, which he really sort of had to when Hank was getting him in and out of bed or the bathtub, he'd be hurting someone who had become not only his helper but his friend.

"Is the wedding still on?" Stefan asked Carolina as she came out of Melanie's bedroom, where she'd been trying on her dress.

"I guess," said Carolina with a shrug. "Maybe it's a good thing the town meeting isn't until after the wedding. That way, if the news is bad, Hank and Mom will already be married. It'll be a done deal!"

Stefan knew how broken up she'd be if she didn't get Hank for a stepfather. She'd never had a father to begin with, not a real one. Once she'd shown Stefan a picture she kept in a book of Robert Louis Stevenson poems. It was a faded snapshot of a teenage boy leaning against the side of an old pickup truck. It was all she had by way of a father.

　　　　　　　　❧

Big Dot had given Melanie a couple of days off to work on the dresses for the wedding, and for one whole day she hardly lifted her head from the ancient treadle sewing machine. It was Carolina's job to keep Trinity out of her hair. She and Stefan tried to teach Trinity how to play Candy Land, but she kept sticking the pieces in her mouth.

The sewing machine clacked away. "Damn!" Melanie would say every once in a while under her breath. It was her strongest curse, and she saved it for special occasions. This was one of them, and she said it often. "Damn!" she said, near tears. "I sewed this whole part on backward!" Carolina rolled her eyes. She didn't have much faith in her mother's sewing skills. But Stefan had begun to feel sorry for Melanie. Even if she was—well, *old* for a bride, it was her first wedding, and she wanted it to be perfect.

"She's wearing white because she's never been married before," Carolina explained later, when they were on their way to the dock to decorate the *Hannah Marie*. Otto was letting a minister perform the ceremony. He said he could do it himself, but it wouldn't be legal. Everybody thought sea captains could marry people, he said, but they really weren't allowed to.

"She isn't really supposed to wear white," Carolina said, frowning. Then she threw her hands up in disgust. "Oh, what does it matter anyway? I mean, is somebody going to come and arrest her or something? Who makes up all these dumb rules anyway?"

Stefan said he sure didn't know.

They were rolling down the creaky wooden pier, headed for the *Hannah Marie*, when Zack came sneaking up behind them, his engine switched off. "Hey!" he said, and they both jumped.

"Hey yourself," Stefan said. Since Zack and Carolina were both behind his chair, he couldn't see if Carolina was happy to see Zack or not. She didn't sound unhappy.

"Get the ramp, will you?" said Carolina as Zack hopped over the rail.

"Huh?" Then he noticed that Stefan just happened to be there. "Oh, okay," he said. He came back with the makeshift ramp, and he and Carolina set it up.

"So," he said to Carolina, "you all excited about the wedding?"

Carolina scuffed the toe of her sneaker against the splintered wood of the deck. "Sure."

"Are you gonna be, you know, like the bridesmaid?"

Stefan figured that Zack didn't know much more about weddings than he did because Carolina had to explain her role as maid of honor, which, she said, wasn't the usual role for a daughter. But in this case mother and daughter were best friends, so it was all right.

"You'd better wear a bag over your head or something," said Zack with a teasing grin.

"A bag?"

"Yeah, so they don't look at you instead of the bride!"

Carolina turned bright red. A panicky look came over her face, and she turned away fast. "Oh, there's Big Dot! She's got all the crepe paper!" She fled down the ramp, leaving Zack and Stefan together on the deck.

"She's a real pretty girl," Zack said. He might have been talking to himself.

"Strong, too," Stefan said.

Zack looked down at Stefan as if he'd just rolled off a spaceship. "Huh?" he said.

〜

The morning of the wedding the little cabin was filled with women, all laughing and talking at the same time. Even Carolina had gotten caught up in the girl stuff, her eyes shining as she watched her mother getting ready to be a bride. Stefan could see that she was waiting for the right moment to give Melanie her wedding present, a pair of pearl earrings. They weren't real pearls exactly, she said when she showed them to Stefan. Could he tell? He said they looked exactly like the ones his mother had, and Carolina beamed.

His mother didn't have any pearls. Or diamonds or rubies for that matter, but Carolina didn't have to know that.

Stefan hung out near the door, pretending to be a world-renowned anthropologist learning about the strange bridal customs of the Amazons. Until he remembered that the Amazons wouldn't have bridal customs, since they didn't have much need for men. He was in the wrong place for sure and hoped that Hank would get there soon.

The men, Melanie had said—meaning Stefan, too—would get ready at Hank's place. Hank wasn't supposed to get even a tiny glimpse of Melanie before the wedding, so she dashed into her bedroom the minute he arrived to pick up Stefan. Stefan could tell by the look on Hank's face that he felt exactly the way Stefan did, surrounded by all those giggling ladies. They got out of there in a hurry, Hank carrying Stefan's suit over one arm.

Hank had told Stefan that they'd stop at Big Dot's for breakfast on the way. Stefan figured, since they'd be sitting right across the table from each other, they were going to have to talk. The whole thing was getting awfully silly anyway. Carolina would pout whenever Hank came into a room. She'd answer him if he asked her a question, but Hank didn't ask a whole lot of questions.

Melanie was fed up with both of them. Be reasonable, she said. She wanted Hank to go with her to Haskells, but Hank knew what she was up to.

"I see trees every day, Mel," he sighed. "Why do I have to go look at trees?"

"You haven't seen these trees, honey," she argued. "These are different. This is an old-growth forest, Hank."

But Melanie was upset with Carolina, too. "You're not being fair, Caro," she said. "Tell him how you feel. You know he'll listen. Refusing to talk to somebody doesn't fix anything, and you know it."

But something had happened to Carolina when she stepped into Haskells Forest for the first time, and she couldn't let it go. The trees had to be saved, no matter what. Loggers were the enemy, and Hank was a logger.

"What good would it do to tell Hank how I feel?" said Carolina, on the verge of tears. "How's that going to change anything?"

Melanie laid her hand over Carolina's. "Maybe it won't change anything, honey. Not at Haskells Forest. But our family is important, too, Carolina. Hank loves you, he loves us all. And he's doing the best he can. He really is."

Carolina must have done some deep thinking after that, because when Hank came to get Stefan, she said, "Hi, Hank!" in a cheery way. She breezed past the two of them on her way out the door. Hank grinned. Then he scratched his head and shrugged. Stefan shrugged back, as if to say he didn't know any more about women than Hank did.

Which was true, of course.

With all the waitresses at Melanie's, Big Dot's was a mess. Hank cleared dirty plates off one of the tables, and he and Stefan sat down to see if somebody would wait on them. When nobody did, he got up and poured two cups of coffee. Stefan wasn't a coffee drinker, but since he was being a man that day, he drank the whole cup, without a drop of cream or sugar.

After a while Charlie, Big Dot's husband and part-time

cook (when she could get him to do it), came shuffling over, wiping his greasy hands on his chef's apron. He took their order without writing it down. Stefan figured they'd be lucky if they got anything, much less the blueberry pancakes and angler's special that they ordered.

Hank and Stefan silently sipped on their coffee for a while, and Stefan could tell Hank wasn't going to start anything up, so he figured he had to. Feeling like a newspaper reporter, he asked Hank if he had any kids of his own. "Two," Hank said. "Boy and a girl." Then he grinned. "Henry Junior and Elizabeth. Beth." So Stefan figured he'd been married before. You *could* have kids, of course, like Melanie did, and not be married, but most people did things in the right order. Melanie would have married Red before she had Trinity, if he'd have married her. But she was lucky he didn't, or she wouldn't have had Hank.

Right about the time Stefan ran out of questions— where Hank was born (Portland), if he ever went to college (nope), what his favorite football team was (Seahawks)— their breakfast came. Hank dived in, but Stefan could see he was thinking about something, working something over in his mind the way a squirrel works an acorn. Stefan could almost see whatever it was swirling around in Hank's gray eyes.

Hank set down his fork, sighed through his nose, peered hard at Stefan across the table, and said, "I never missed a child support payment, Bud. Not once. My ex, she needed a car? I bought her one. Now she's sick. Lung cancer. Needs somebody to come in, help her with things. That costs, too, you know."

Stefan didn't really know, and so he just listened. Hank had gotten himself all wound up. Half the time he talked to the table; the other half he looked straight into Stefan's eyes. Hank's were so full of sadness Stefan wanted to look away.

"Sure, I could say I done my part. Paid for the kids' college, gave my ex the house. But"—he shrugged his big shoulders—"I don't know how to say it exactly. We're still family is what." He picked up his fork again and looked at it as if he were trying to figure out what to do with it. "My ex and me, Mary Alice her name is, we don't get along, not even now, but we're still . . . connected. Yeah," he sighed, "we're still connected." And then he hurried to explain, in case Stefan didn't understand. "It's not that I don't love Melanie and the girls. I do. And I'll do right by them, too."

"I know you will," Stefan said. He was sorry he had made Hank talk so much. He could see it wasn't easy for him.

"But you don't walk away from the things that count," he said. "You can't do that."

Stefan tried to think of something he could say, man to man, but nothing he could come up with from only thirteen years of living seemed like the right thing. Hank was a hero. Not the kind that rode off into the sunset, but the one who stayed behind and took care of business.

Hank lifted his big rough hands. "What I'm trying to say is that I need the work. It's all I know how to do."

"Oh," Stefan said.

"I know you think we shouldn't be cutting down the old trees. You and Carolina, and now Melanie, too. But what else have I got to do, Stefan? You tell me that."

Stefan couldn't.

11

"WELCOME to Casa La Grunge," said Dean, bowing in the doorway to room number six at the Pinetop Motel and Apartments. Dean's dark hair was all slicked back, and he was wearing a shiny black eye patch that matched the black checks in his black-and-yellow sports jacket.

While Hank showered and shaved in the bathroom, Dean and Stefan played gin rummy on the nightstand between Stefan's chair and one of the beds.

"Hank's a good man," Dean said when he'd won the first three games and was shuffling for the fourth. "That Melanie's one lucky lady."

Carolina would have expected Stefan to put in something for her mom, but he did it on his own anyway. "That Melanie's a good woman," he drawled, imitating Dean's midwestern twang.

Dean stopped shuffling the cards and gave Stefan a sharp

look. Then he laughed. "Yep, yep, she is. You're right, son." He dealt the cards, chuckling to himself. "And you like ol' Carolina, too, don'tcha?"

Stefan pretended not to know what Dean was hinting at. "Yes, sir," he said. "We're best friends."

"Best friends," Dean mused, fanning out his cards and squinting at them with his one good eye. "Huh! Best friends. You're how old?"

"Thirteen, sir." Behind Dean's head, hanging on the wall, was the world's ugliest painting of a trout doing a back flip.

"Yeah . . . thirteen, yeah." Dean set down a fan of royalty, and Stefan could see he was on his way to another win. " 'Bout time you started talking about *girl*friends, kiddo. You thought much about that?"

Stefan was warming up inside the dark blue wool suit Hank had helped him change into. He loosened his striped tie. "Sure," he said stoutly. Then his voice cracked. "I mean, who doesn't?"

It was true, he'd done some thinking. But he didn't have things figured out, not at all. He knew it would be different for him if he had a girlfriend. Different than for other guys. But he didn't know exactly how. His body did all the dumb embarrassing things it was supposed to do at his age— "saluting the flag" was how his father put it—but most girls didn't even see him as a guy because of the chair, so what did it matter? It was better not to think too much about how it would all work out with a girl (or wouldn't) until he absolutely had to.

And he didn't want to think about it now, even if it was the kind of day that made you think about how it could be you getting married someday. And anyway, he and Carolina were too young. She'd much rather catch a fish or climb a tree than kiss a boy, he was pretty sure about that.

"Gin," Dean said, "with my card." He set down three cards and then the last, a one-eyed jack. "You'd better watch that motorcycle fella," he said, squinting at Stefan through a steady stream of smoke that rose from an overflowing ashtray perched on the edge of the bed.

"Zack?" Stefan squeaked, as if there were a dozen other guys on Harleys hanging around Haskells Bay.

"Gonna get your girl if you don't watch him."

"She's not, like, my girl," Stefan said. His face was red and hot by then. What was taking Hank so long?

"Well, she won't be if that kid gets his way. Gotta take care of business, my man," Dean said with a sorry shake of his head, "gotta take care of business," right as Hank came out of the bedroom. Dean let out a low whistle, and Hank grinned with all the teeth he had. In his dark gray suit and bright green tie, he was looking sharp. He'd even trimmed back his wild red beard for the occasion.

"I can't get my feet into these pointy-toed shoes," he said, holding a pair of black dress shoes by the tips of his fingers. "I gotta wear my boots."

They all looked down at Hank's big white feet. Dean frowned. "Better boots than them ugly feet is how I see it."

≈

The *Hannah Marie* looked like a bride herself, an old fat bride. White crepe paper had been strung through all her lines and dripped over her rails. There were white and silver balloons everywhere, even in the fishing net. Somebody had set a garden trellis next to the wheelhouse, and that was decorated, too, with white roses and ribbons that fluttered in the onshore morning breeze. People had gathered in clumps of two or three on the deck or on the pier below. Stefan didn't see Carolina or Melanie, but he knew that brides hid out until the last minute so they could make a grand appearance.

Then he saw Zack. Zack was wearing a dark gray suit that made him look like James Bond.

Stefan wasn't in the wedding party. But Hank had stuck a white carnation in his lapel, like the one he and Dean wore, and Stefan felt like part of the wedding.

And then he noticed that the ramp had been set up. In all the rush and excitement of getting ready, Carolina had made sure he could get aboard. She'd been thinking about him, just as he'd been thinking about her. He felt a true part of things then.

The invited guests hung around, strangers and friends all dressed up, trying to think of things to talk about. Stefan heard one of the ladies say that the bride was going to be happy because the sun was out, or something like that. Another asked if Melanie's first husband had died or if she was divorced, which didn't seem like the right thing to talk about at a wedding. Nobody seemed to have the answer anyway, and Hank and Stefan weren't telling.

Finally, when everybody was about to melt inside their suits and fancy dresses, Otto came out of the wheelhouse wearing a moth-eaten pinstriped gangster suit and a bright red tie. He looked around at everybody as if he couldn't figure out how they all got on his boat. Then he seemed to remember who was captain and took charge. "Over here," he ordered Hank. "You," he said to Dean. "Over here." The two men stood like stone-faced bookends, one on each side of the garden trellis. Otto even told the minister where to stand, and the minister listened.

Over a blaring loudspeaker came the tinny sound of the wedding march. And before Stefan was ready, before he knew what was happening, Carolina stepped out of the wheelhouse. His breath stuck in his throat, and when he remembered to breathe again, it was as if a hundred mayflies had hatched at once and were flying around in his chest. Later, when he was home again and trying to describe how she looked to his mother, he had none of the right words.

Her long dress was a shimmery pale blue, he said, almost white, and it didn't have a lot of ruffles or bows or anything. It was kind of plain, but not plain. Kind of low-cut, but not really. It didn't have sleeves, and it fit her snug around the waist. It was a dress a girl like Carolina should wear. An honest kind of dress, he ended up saying.

For the first time since coming to get Stefan at the airport, she wore her hair out of its usual ponytail, cascading like tumbling water onto her shoulders. Light blue and white ribbons were threaded through it. Her blushing face matched her lip gloss, but she grinned bravely at everybody, holding her little bouquet.

He could have said that she was every bit as pretty in her rubber jumper, but it wouldn't have been true. That was just talk for the movies.

Here Comes the Bride, blared the tinny speaker, and Melanie stepped out in her white wedding dress, holding Trinity's hand. Stefan was a little worried that one of Melanie's sleeves might fall off, but she wasn't worried about a thing. He could see that by the way she smiled at Carolina and Hank. The time she took doing that, looking at them and beaming, gave Stefan goose bumps. Trinity hid within the folds of Melanie's long white dress and peered out shyly. She was dressed all in pink, right down to her shiny pink shoes.

Things got very quiet as the minister began the ceremony. The words were so serious, Stefan wondered why they didn't always stick. All those promises about loving and honoring until the very end—until death. It gave him the chills. It seemed like a long time before Melanie and Hank got pronounced husband and wife, but they kissed a long time, too, while everybody cheered like mad.

A hiss and pop of champagne corks, and the men began peeling out of their suit jackets. Melanie went around hugging everybody she could get her hands on. Carolina stuck Trinity on her hip and came over to Stefan. "Cool, huh?" she said, all smiles.

"Very cool," he agreed, struck again by how beautiful Carolina was. He tried to blot out Zack, who was standing on top of the wheelhouse with his fists on his skinny hips, like Captain Bligh. His eyes were like radar, following Carolina's every move. "Your mom looks so happy," Stefan said.

"She is!" said Carolina. "I've never seen her so happy."

Hank brought Carolina and Stefan plastic cups half filled with champagne. "For the toast," he said, grinning, "but that's all you get."

As best man, Dean gave the toast. He rambled on and on like a standup comic with a bad script while people stood holding their cups in the air, waiting for him to finish. Finally somebody broke in, "Let's drink to the old bride and groom!" which didn't sound quite right either but did the trick. They clicked their plastic cups and cheered. Carolina choked on the bubbles.

Out of the corner of his eye, he saw Zack climb down off the wheelhouse. "Party time!" he cried, waving a bottle of champagne.

12

CONGRATULATIONS HANK AND MELANIE, said a long white banner over the door to Big Dot's. The stuffed fish were still hanging on the walls, but all the tables were covered with white tablecloths and flowers, and had been moved closer together to make space for a tiny dance floor. Silver and white balloons hung in a bunch from a light fixture, and white crepe paper crisscrossed the ceiling.

As the wedding party came through the door, Melanie and Hank in front, the band struck up "Here Comes the Bride," but the song was better this time because it was live—even though the band was only one person with a rickety electric piano and a drum machine. Melanie's eyes sparkled as if she'd never seen the room before, as if she'd forgotten all the fishburgers and greasy french fries she'd delivered to those same exact tables.

The wedding dinner was potluck, everybody bringing something, even if it was only a six-pack of beer. The food covered four tables: fried chicken, smoked salmon, potato salad, Jell-O molds. The wedding party went first, so it was a while before Stefan got to fill his plate and take it back to the table.

And there was Zack, not bothering with the food at all. His hand was still wrapped around the champagne bottle, and it didn't look as if he'd shared much of what was inside with anybody else. He had the faraway, stupid sort of smile on his face that people get when they think they're supercool but have only had too much to drink.

Stefan waited like a kid on Christmas for Zack to start making a real fool out of himself. Which didn't take long. Bottle in hand, Zack went swaggering across the floor straight up to Dean. Stefan couldn't hear what Zack said, but whatever it was made Dean and the other loggers laugh. Zack gave Dean a shove. Dean looked like he wanted to punch Zack right in the nose, but he used his mouth instead of his fists. The loggers howled, slapping their knees. Zack slunk away, a murderous look on his face.

To Stefan's chagrin, Carolina wasn't there to see the great Zack humiliated—she had taken Trinity to the rest room. What timing! Stefan sat alone, hoping Zack had left for good. He couldn't wait to tell Carolina what happened.

But if he told her, wouldn't she just feel sorry for Zack?

Now Carolina was back and had Trinity on her lap, trying to get her to eat something besides chocolate kisses. One of the pale blue ribbons in Carolina's hair was hanging by a thread. He knew that what he was about to do next was pretty stupid, but he did it anyway. He slipped the ribbon from her hair without her knowing and wrapped it around his little finger.

But someone had been watching. Twisting around, Stefan saw Zack wink as if they shared some dirty little secret.

People had begun to dance, the guy on the electric piano banging away for all he was worth. Hank had swooped Trinity off Carolina's lap and was dancing with Trinity and Melanie at the same time, stomping around in his logger's boots as if he knew what he was doing.

"Come on, Carolina."

Carolina and Stefan turned at the same time. Zack was holding out his hand. "Come on," he said, with a nod at the packed dance floor, "let's dance."

Carolina's eyes widened. "Um, no thanks," she said.

"Why not?" Zack looked surprised, as if he couldn't imagine why anybody would ever turn him down.

"I, um, I don't know how to do that kind of stuff." She laughed, watching her mother and Hank twirling and stomping.

"Hey! Who does? Come on!"

Carolina looked at Stefan for just a second, and then at Zack again, and in that second Stefan saw all the things that made Carolina such a special girl. She wanted to dance with Zack—any fool could have seen that. But there was Stefan, her best friend in the whole world, and he couldn't dance. Carolina wouldn't have hurt his feelings for anything. She'd have sat there all evening, right by Stefan's side if he'd wanted her to. And had a good time, too. But there was more to it than that:

If she *didn't* dance because he *couldn't* dance, then she'd be doing the worst thing; she'd be making him different.

Carolina hesitated a few seconds more, then held out her hand to Zack. Stefan watched them walk side by side to the dance floor, the tall good-looking boy in the slim dark gray suit and Carolina, the fairy princess. To admit to himself all the things that were going through his mind right then would have made him feel pretty small. And he was trying, as his father would have said, to be big about it. With a sunken heart, Stefan watched slick L.A. Zack twirl Carolina, *his* Carolina, as if she were a fragile little doll in a jewelry box, and he tried his best to be big about it.

It was worse later when the lights went down and the one-man band began to play the slow numbers. When Stefan saw Zack put his hand on Carolina's back and bring her close, he spun Grandpa's wheels and headed out of there.

Big Dot's porch was empty, but the parking lot was full. Stefan counted all the cars, just for something to do. Twenty-six. And one big black motorcycle. He was feeling pretty sorry for himself, but angry, too, which was how he sometimes got when he didn't know who to blame. Like for the fact that he couldn't hop down off Big Dot's porch by himself and go home, for example, or dance with a girl. He knew it wasn't anybody's fault. Not his folks', not that of the doctor who delivered him, and certainly not Carolina's. But he sat there and stewed anyway, wishing he could read Carolina's mind and then knowing he wouldn't really want to do that, even if he could.

A half-moon hung in a black, black sky. An owl hooted in the trees across the road, and Stefan figured that it was alone, too, because it hooted several more times and never got an answer. Everybody was pairing up that night, or trying to.

"Stefan?" Carolina said in her shimmery dress. "What are you doing out here?"

"Just taking a breather," he said, an old movie line that popped into his head.

Carolina's eyes went to the ribbon on Stefan's finger, and her hand went up quickly to her hair. Stefan slid his hand under his leg, his face burning.

"Stefan?" she said, as if she weren't quite sure it was really her good old friend Stefan there on the porch.

"Breathing," he said. "I'm just breathing."

"Oh," she said, uncertainly. "Well, it is getting pretty hot inside."

"Pretty hot," he drawled.

Carolina gave him a funny look. "What's wrong?"

"Wrong? Nothing." And he really tried then not to be a jerk. Not to let his bad mood ruin a very special night for her.

"It's Zack, isn't it?" she said with a sad little sigh. "You don't like him very much, do you?"

He opened his mouth to say something, but nothing came out.

Carolina kept looking at Stefan. "Come back inside, Stefan," she said softly. "I won't dance anymore."

A fist squeezed his heart. Of all things, not that! "What? No! Carolina, I—"

"Come on, silly. They're going to cut the cake." She put her hands on the chair to turn Stefan around, but for once she asked first: "Okay?"

"Okay," he said because it was what she wanted. And then: "Carolina?"

"I'm not falling for that one again," she said, laughing.

"No, really," he said.

"What then?"

"I'm sorry," he said. "I'm sorry for being such a poop."

"You're not a poop," she said. Now she wasn't laughing. "You're my best friend, same as always!"

But for the first time in the nearly three years that they had known each other, it wasn't the same, and they both knew it.

13

"I'LL just bet he's going to stand us up!" said Carolina. The flyer had read 7 p.m., but it was ten to eight and the owner of Coastal Lumber had not yet appeared for the promised town meeting. Carolina kept twisting around in her chair to watch the door. If the infamous Mr. Farnsworth really had bloody fangs and horns or a forked tail, she wanted to be the first to see them. Then she began to fidget, pulling on Stefan's arm to ask him something, as if he knew everything there was to know about the ecosystem of planet Earth.

Big Dot's was full of noisy, restless townspeople, fishermen, lumbermen, cranky kids, and all the rest, waiting for the meeting to begin. There was a kind of rumble in the room, like a train coming from a long way off. Whichever way things went, somebody was going to be unhappy.

Everything started out wrong. Hank wasn't sitting at their table. At first he stood next to it, shuffling from one foot to the other, hanging his thumbs in his suspenders and looking like he'd rather be in jail than in that room. Then he was back against the wall. Later, Stefan glimpsed his red beard at a table up front full of noisy loggers. Dean's voice rose above the rest. "Done deal!" he said a couple of times, as if he knew already what was going to be.

Then, at five past eight, a short balding man in a gray business suit appeared in the doorway. He nodded once to the left, once to the right, and made his way to the front of the room. Three men in dark business suits followed, gliding like Secret Service behind the President. They stood in a line at parade rest, facing the audience, their eyes on the back wall.

A lady with curly bluish hair shot out of her seat and went to a microphone that had been set up on the front table. It shrieked whenever she tried to speak into it, and finally she gave up and hollered instead. "I'm Mrs. Albert Albemarle, your mayor," she yelled, "for the benefit of y'all who don't know me."

"Go, Annie!" shouted a voice from the back of the room. The mayor shot a teacher's look in the direction of the voice, cleared her throat, and continued.

"This here's an important meeting for Haskells Bay," she shouted, "and I think it would be most appropriate if we started with a prayer for guidance. Reverend Burns?"

The minister stood, and hats came off around the room. "Our Heavenly Father," he thundered in a voice that didn't need a mike, "the town of Haskells Bay has a colorful and illustrious history . . ." Stefan thought they were in for a long one then, but instead of telling God the history of Haskells Bay (which He had to know anyway), the minister asked for some help in making the right decision and said, "Amen."

Then the mayor introduced Mr. Gerald Farnsworth, who never once glanced at the mike. The man on his right had grabbed it up. "Testing," he spat into it. "Testing." The mike shrieked, and people covered their ears. Mr. Farnsworth leaned over and said something to his right-hand man, whose voice was whiny as a buzz saw. "I will be speaking on behalf of Mr. Farnsworth," the man said, and that's just what he did, avoiding the shrieks as best he could. Mr. Farnsworth told him what he wanted to say, a few sentences at a time, and his right-hand man, in his whiny buzz-saw voice, re-peated them to the crowd.

They started with all the positive things. Jobs, and a boost in the economy for Haskells Bay. "There will be more jobs in lumber than you folks will be able to fill," the right-hand man said. "Your town will experience a rebirth as never before."

"We ain't dead yet!" yelled Otto, who appeared in the doorway, swaying from side to side. "Leastways not till you come in and kill us first!" His face was red, and there was rage in his drunken, watery blue eyes. He was about to stum-ble past Stefan's table and head for the front of the room when Big Dot grabbed his arm.

"Sit down and shut up, you old fool," she spat. Snatching away his bottle, she handed it over to the first person she saw, who happened to be Stefan.

"Here, Stefan, I'll take that," said Melanie. She set the bottle of whiskey on the floor out of Otto's sight.

But Otto had plenty more to say. "Tell us what you're gonna do about the fish, huh? Why don't you tell us about that!"

Big Dot gave Otto's arm a good shake. "That's enough," she said. Otto swayed in his chair. He kept on muttering, but not loud enough for the men in front to hear. Big Dot could be real scary when she wanted to be. She was the only person in town that Otto had any respect for.

When Otto had settled down, more or less, the right-hand man looked uncertainly at his boss to find out what to say next. Mr. Farnsworth spoke into his ear, and the right-hand man continued. "Some . . . *adjustments* will have to be made," he said. "That's the way it is in every small town on the move."

Things began stirring up then. There were plenty of people who'd heard enough. "Adjustments! Well, if that don't beat all!"

"Let's take a vote! You can't push your way in here and cut down all our trees!"

"Yeah! Yeah! Who invited you here anyway!"

Then the loggers started in on the fishermen and the "eco-Nazis," as they called anybody who tried to defend the environment. "You're a bunch of stupid idiots! Can't you see we need this work? How are we supposed to feed our families with the lumber industry dying? Mr. Farnsworth is right. It's Haskells Forest or nothing!"

"I'll shut your mouth for you, you—" Otto shook off Big Dot's arm and headed for the front of the room, for the loggers or maybe for Mr. Farnsworth himself. He was steady and quick for someone so old and so drunk. Everybody but Stefan stood up to watch what was going on down front. Stefan heard some thuds and groans—*pow, thud, ooph,* just like in the cartoons—and everybody yelling at once.

"What's going on?" he asked Carolina, who had scampered up to the top of the table.

"Hank's got him in an armlock!" she said. "Uh-oh! He got away! Dean's got him now!"

At last things quieted down, and when the people sat again, Stefan could see that Hank and Dean had a good hold on Otto, who was running out of steam. He looked like a tired old walrus, and Stefan couldn't help feeling sorry for him.

"The old man's right," said a fisherman from his seat. His wife gave him a poke, and he stood up, clearing his throat. "Everywhere you guys log, the fish go belly up. Straight down the coast, it's the same thing!"

Another fisherman stood up, then another: "Yeah! What do you care about what happens to Haskells Bay? Sure, there will be jobs. For a while! Then you'll head out, and we'll be worse off than before!"

"Yeah!"

"Yeah!"

Then the loggers started in, and for a tense moment it looked as if there might be an all-out brawl.

The four men in suits stood silently by, bored, and Stefan began to think they'd done all this before in other small towns and knew right from the first what would happen, how people would react, and that none of it mattered. Farnsworth would do what he would do.

"Mr. Farnsworth would like to remind you," the right-hand man said, "that he does not have to be here. He has come in the spirit of generosity, as a new member of your . . . community, and is willing to hear what you have to say. If," he repeated, "if you can conduct yourselves like civilized adults."

"Who does he think he is!" sniffed a woman at the next table. "Yeah!" said another, but they looked a bit embarrassed. After a little while a fisherman stood, politely removed his cap, and in a calm, adult voice asked if Coastal Lumber would be building a paper mill, "the way they did up north where all the fish died."

Grumble, rumble from the fishermen.

The right-hand man knew the answer to that one. There was no "immediate plan" for a paper mill, he said, stressing the "immediate."

Two elderly ladies, identical twins dressed in matching tweed jackets and red-rimmed glasses, stood up at the same time. "We are Lila and Leela Barnes," they said. In a wavering voice, Lila (or Leela) said that it wasn't fair, wasn't right, to cut down all the beautiful trees, that God Himself would cry watching them do that. They were birders vacationing in the area, Leela (or Lila) said. "Lifelong birders." Did the gentlemen have any idea how many species of birds lived in that forest?

The four men looked blank. The right-hand man cleared his throat. "I am certain Mr. Farnsworth is familiar with his bird species," he said finally. He looked at his boss, who nodded.

His birds! Stefan, who'd forgotten he'd once felt the same way about Crow, couldn't believe it.

"Mr. Farnsworth's counted all the trees himself, right?" wisecracked the kid who worked the counter in Haskells Bay Sodas and Sundries.

"Exactly how many trees are you going to cut down?" said the librarian in her clear no-nonsense voice.

"Ma'am," said the right-hand man, not even bothering to translate Mr. Farnsworth anymore. He knew his lines. "For every tree that is harvested, two will be planted in its place. There will be no shortage of trees in Haskells Bay, not now and certainly not in the future."

"Stefan!" hissed Carolina. "Tell them about the old growth! Tell them it's not the same!"

Dean stood up. "I just wanted to say that trees are, well, trees! You can't eat 'em, and you can't pay rent with 'em unless you cut them down. I'm speakin' for all of us loggers here when I say thank you. Thanks, Coastal Lumber!"

The loggers all cheered. Dean held up his hand for a high five, and Hank gave him one.

"Tell them, Stefan!" Carolina urged, pulling on his sleeve.

To Stefan and Carolina's surprise, Melanie stood up. She licked her lips nervously. "I was thinking," she began in her soft southern accent, and her eyes met Hank's surprised ones. "Couldn't y'all start somewhere else? Like a place farther down the coast that isn't already a town?" She looked once, quickly, around the room then. "Have any of you gone to the forest? I mean, inside it? It's, well, it's a magical place. Those trees are hundreds of years old, older than anything in this town. I'm sorry, but . . ." She shrugged once helplessly and sat down. Stefan guessed she was apologizing to Hank.

Carolina grabbed her mother's hand and squeezed it. They said with their eyes all the things too hard to say with words. The room got very quiet then. Stefan could feel Carolina waiting.

But his hand just wouldn't go up. Since talking with Hank the morning of the wedding, he'd done a lot of thinking about the loggers. Most of them, like Hank, had only their lumbering skills to make a living, to support their families. Their fathers had been loggers, and before them, their grandfathers. It was a way of life in the Northwest, and until lately, nobody had questioned it.

As different as the fishermen were from the loggers, it was the same for them. They fished because they'd grown up next to the ocean, and boats were closer to the way they thought and felt than anything on land.

There were Melanie and Carolina, who loved Hank but loved the big trees, too. And Big Dot, whose best customers had always been fishermen.

Most of all there was Haskells Forest, which towered over everybody, making them feel like the intruders they were.

And then there was Stefan Millington Crouch III, a rich brat from out of state who thought he had something to say because he loved wildlife, maybe more than people. But he cared about Hank, too, and he cared about logger families and fisher families. How could he not?

It was time to muck around inside himself to see what it was he really believed, no matter what anybody else thought, and then get ready to stand up for it. Even if he ended up standing all by himself. Even if he was sitting. In other words, it was one of the worst hard times.

The only good thing about it was that Zack wasn't anywhere to be seen.

"Mr. Farnsworth wishes to remind you," said the right-hand man, as the mike let out an ear-splitting screech, "that Haskells Forest is private property. *His* private property, which means of course that he has the right to do whatever he wants with it."

"Get it over with!" growled somebody in the front row. "When are you moving in?"

"Our target date is August fourteenth," said the right-hand man.

The whole room seemed to gasp, as if all the air had been sucked right out of it. "August fourteenth?" said the mayor, jumping to her feet. "But that's next week!"

Farnsworth's men waited until the cheers and curses settled. "Mr. Farnsworth would like to thank you all for coming," the right-hand man said. The owner of Coastal Lumber nodded once at the audience. Then the four men went single file toward the door, Farnsworth at the end of the line.

"I'll kill you, you greedy son of—" sputtered Otto with his last gasp of steam. He made a weak lunge for Farnsworth, who shook him off like an insect. Everybody in the audience turned to watch the four suit backs glide through the door and evaporate into the night.

"Well, that's it," said Melanie with a deep, sad sigh. She stood up, shifting Trinity, who'd fallen asleep against her shoulder. Carolina turned and stalked out of the room.

Melanie looked at Stefan with raised eyebrows.

Stefan shrugged as if he didn't know why Carolina had left them behind, but he did. He knew because he was thinking exactly what she was thinking. Stefan Millington Crouch III was all talk. But not when it mattered. When it mattered, he just let everybody else do the talking. Even Melanie had spoken up for the forest, though every logger in town and every logger's wife would call her a traitor.

Stefan Millington Crouch III had sat like a bump on a log, a log he didn't deserve.

～

They all turned in early that night, nobody wanting to talk about what had happened and how soon the forest would be gone. Even Hank, who was relieved to have the work, looked miserable. Carolina stomped out to the bus without saying good night. There was a lump in Stefan's throat the size of a dinosaur egg as he lay in her bed, looking out through the window at a sky filled with an explosion of stars.

It had all happened so fast. There had been that one

minute, less than a minute, when his hand should have gone straight up and didn't. And then the minute was over. Melanie had stood up then, almost as if she had to. Maybe because Stefan didn't. And he was ashamed. As proud as he was of her, that's how ashamed he was of himself.

All he knew for sure, lying in Carolina's narrow bed, was that he'd let the chance go by, and he would never get it back. He'd let his best friend down. She'd never believe in him again. He'd let a whole forest down. He'd have kicked himself if he could.

14

CAROLINA and Stefan tried hard to pretend everything was the same between them, but something, something they had only felt but never talked about, had changed. Part of Carolina was somewhere else. It was only a small part, but to Stefan the space between them felt like a chasm, and he began to sulk inside, where she couldn't see.

A day passed, then another. Like water through his fingers, his time with Carolina was slipping away. He could do nothing to make it right between them, and neither could she. Trying hard to reclaim what had been—before Zack, and before the town meeting—they did all the usual things. They took long walks, hung out at the dock, played their favorite games, and worried themselves sick over what would become of Haskells Forest. It seemed just the same, but it wasn't.

They were sitting in Haskells Bay Sodas and Sundries

sharing their favorite chocolate-caramel sundae when, just as if they had been waiting for him, in came Zack.

"Hey, pretty girl," he said. Carolina gave him a quick grin and looked down at her broken fingernails. Stefan glowered like a storm cloud on the horizon, but Zack acted the way he always did, as if Stefan weren't even there.

Zack had a lot to say about Haskells Forest, even though he hadn't been at the meeting. "Aw, come on," he said when Carolina told him about the target date, "you knew what was going to happen. Everybody did."

"Maybe we needed to hear it for ourselves," Carolina said sadly.

Zack pulled out a chair and slouched into it. "You didn't really think you were going to change their minds, did ya?" He gave Carolina a half-grin, his trademark. He was wearing cologne. Stefan's appetite melted into the soup of the sundae.

"I don't know if their minds could be changed." Carolina frowned. "But we had to try." She glanced at Stefan, traitor to the cause. "It's all happening so fast. I still can't believe it! I can't believe we're all just going to stand by while those trees are—are *slaughtered*!" Carolina's cheeks were bright pink, which is how they got whenever she was worked up about something, or so Stefan told himself. It didn't have to be because of Zack. "You should go there, Zack," she said more softly. "You should go to Haskells Forest and see the trees for yourself, like Melanie said. Everybody should. Especially now."

"Oh, I've been there," Zack said casually.

"You have?"

"Sure. A bunch of times." He slung his dark hair out of his eyes with a shake of his head. It was something he did whenever he lied or needed to feel important.

"Well then, you know!" she said. "You know how beautiful it is. How important those trees are."

"Sure." He shrugged.

"Well, I don't see how you can be so calm about it," she said, her old self again, challenging Zack as if he were just anybody, "if you've actually been there. Don't you want to do something?"

Zack sighed as if he were about a hundred years old. Then he leaned across the table until his nose was almost touching Carolina's, or so it appeared from where Stefan sat. Carolina's face turned a brighter pink, and beads of sweat popped out on her forehead. "Yeah, I want to do something. Who says I don't? Just because I didn't go to some dumb meeting—"

"It wasn't a dumb meeting, Zack," Stefan said, speaking up for the first time, trying his best to get those noses apart. "It was a chance for people, the people who *live* here, to have a say about what's going to happen to their town." He tried not to think about the birder twins who didn't live in Haskells Bay but had spoken up anyway.

Zack's eyes glazed over as Stefan tried to tell him how important it was for people to have their say, feeling more and more like a hypocrite with every word.

"We can still do a protest march, right?" said Carolina. "You could organize it, Zack, since you know all about that kind of stuff."

"The stuff in L.A. was *big*," drawled Zack. "Guerrilla warfare. It wasn't some silly little march, Carolina. Anyway, it's too late for a protest." Zack brushed some dust off his jeans.

"No, it isn't! It's not too late until the last tree is gone."

"Nah," said Zack. "If you want to stop them from cutting down trees, you've got to do more than march around with a couple of signs."

"What?" said Carolina. "What can we do?"

"There's things," Zack said mysteriously.

❧

Stefan and Carolina baby-sat Trinity most afternoons, teaching her how to play games that were too old for her. It gave them an excuse to play Chutes and Ladders, which they still liked, even if it was a baby game.

"I'll be yellow," Stefan said, choosing his marker—then nearly swallowed his tongue.

But Carolina didn't catch on. "That's okay, I wanna be red anyway. Trinity, you can be green."

"Wed!" demanded Trinity, and put the blue marker in her mouth.

"Okay, be red," said Carolina. "But you can't eat the pieces."

"Lallo!" Trinity cleared the board with her foot, sending pieces flying everywhere.

"Trinity, behave!" Carolina almost never raised her voice to Trinity, whose eyes widened with surprise.

"It doesn't matter how we play, Carolina," Stefan said.

"Let her just, you know, push the pieces around the board. Get the hang of it."

"Well, she'll never learn that way!"

"Who cares? It's just a game!"

"I care, that's who! She's my sister, and I want her to learn stuff!"

"But she's a baby—"

"Oh, what do you know anyway? She's not your sis—" Carolina clapped a hand over her mouth. "Oh, Stefan, I'm so sorry!"

"No problemo," Stefan said, southern California style, but he meant it. He and Carolina hadn't talked about Heather for a long time, not since Carolina had come to live with the Crouches and slept in Heather's room. Stefan didn't have a sister anymore, it was true. Except in his memory— his big sister would always be there.

They were quiet for a while, watching Trinity line up all the pieces in the middle of the board. "One, two, fwee . . ."

"Why didn't you say something at the meeting, Stefan?" Carolina said suddenly, in the sad, quiet voice that was worse, far worse than her angry one. But it was almost a relief to have it out. "All that research we did, and you just clammed up!"

"Well, so did you," Stefan said with a shrug. It was true, even if it didn't answer her question.

"But you're the one—" she said. "You're the one who *knows* all the stuff!"

"You know as much as I do."

She blinked. "Well, maybe. Maybe I do now, but . . ."

"But what?"

She was stuck. "Time for your nap, Trinity." She scooped Trinity up off the floor and took her into her room.

When she came back, Carolina slumped onto the sofa, her long legs in their faded, torn jeans dangling over the side. "You're right," she said, "I could have said something. I could have explained what happens when you chop down an old-growth forest."

"So could I," Stefan said miserably, "but I didn't."

Then Stefan told Carolina about the talk he had had with Hank at Big Dot's the morning of the wedding, how much Hank was counting on the work. "Then when Melanie stood up and said what she did, even though people were never going to understand . . ." Stefan shook his head, unable to put the rest into words.

"She says what she believes. That's the way it is."

"But she believes in Hank, too. That's just the problem. You can believe in more than one thing, but you have to choose anyway. It sucks!"

"Yup." She grinned, and so did Stefan. They were back on even ground.

"I'm sorry," Stefan said. "I'm sorry I let you down."

Carolina's green eyes narrowed. "You didn't let me down, Stefan. What's it got to do with me? This is between you and, well, *you*."

❧

While they were putting Chutes and Ladders back together, Trinity yelled out that she needed a "dink a wawa." Carolina told her that she didn't need a drink of water, she needed to close her eyes and go to sleep. Then Trinity said she needed a "gwass a mik. Chokit mik!" This time Carolina ignored her.

"Let's organize a protest," Stefan said.

"You and me?"

Did she really think he'd want to include Zack? "Sure. Why not? We can start by putting up flyers for a meeting. Find out who's interested."

"Do you think it'll work?"

Stefan said he didn't know, but that he wanted to do something.

"Oh, me too, Stefan! Wait, I'll get some stuff to make a flyer." She came back with a soup can full of colored pens and a bunch of computer paper. "Can you draw trees?"

"Sure," he said. "Trees are easy!"

They made a flyer, Carolina carefully lettering the announcement and Stefan drawing trees that looked like giant mushrooms. "We can photocopy a bunch more at the post office," she said. "But we have to write where the meeting will be. Big Dot's?"

"What about here?"

Carolina looked hesitantly around the small room. "Well, I don't think we'd better. Now that Hank lives with us, it doesn't seem fair." She thought a moment. "I know!" she said. "We'll have it on the bus! Then it's really ours. Something we did without, you know, the grownups."

"Cool," Stefan said.

"Oh, Stefan, do you think it'll make any difference?"

He didn't. What he thought and didn't want to say was that Zack was probably right: A bunch of protesters didn't stand a chance against a giant company. But by then he'd begun to understand that it wasn't what finally happened that mattered the most, but how you got to what finally happened, and what you did to get there.

"I don't know if it'll make any difference, Carolina," he admitted. "But we have to try."

"I knew you'd think of something." She beamed, as if it had all been Stefan's idea from the beginning. "You always do."

15

THE first and only meeting of Save Haskells Trees took place on Carolina's bus, transformed into headquarters. Carolina and Stefan spent two days painting the outside, and now the bus was covered with sayings like FORESTS ARE FOREVER and STOP KILLING THE TREES. While Carolina painted the high parts, standing on a ladder, Stefan painted his famous giant mushroom trees, along with some V-shaped flying birds, doggy-looking bears, and stick-figure kids having picnics. Trinity "helped."

When Hank came out to put Stefan on the painted-up bus, he just shook his head, picked up the chair and Stefan all in one piece, and wordlessly stowed him aboard.

Eight people showed up to save the forest. Two of them turned around and left when they saw that a couple of kids were in charge, even though Carolina introduced Stefan as a "naturalist-in-training boy genius."

Stefan didn't think that helped much.

Big Dot and the head waitress, Evelyn, came. So did the birder twins, the librarian, and Melanie. Fortunately, Big Dot's was closed on Mondays, or they'd have only had the birders and the librarian.

And Zack. As the meeting was about to start, up he roared on the Harley, and down went Stefan's mood.

Carolina announced that Stefan would explain the plan, which he did. Starting the next day, he said, they would try to have at least two people (they'd hoped for six) in three different shifts, holding signs at the place where the forest began. One sign would say, "Honk if you love big trees," just to gauge what kind of support they had. They had only three days to rally the people of Haskells Bay. Others would surely join in once they saw what was happening. Their little group would just have to start things going.

"I think it's a good plan," said the librarian, whose name was Mary Trout, "but I can't take all that time off from work. I'll keep my sign next to the checkout desk and try and talk people into joining up."

Big Dot and Evelyn volunteered for the early shift. "Charlie can set up for breakfast," said Big Dot, with a firm nod of her chin. Evelyn rolled her eyes.

Lila (or was it Leela?) Barnes spoke up next. "My sister and I think we should do our shifts together," she said. "Otherwise it might appear that there is only one person doing two different shifts."

Everybody agreed.

Zack leaned against the wall of the bus, his arms crossed, the usual smirk on his face.

"What about you, Zack?" Stefan said.

"Nah," Zack answered, exactly as Stefan expected. "I'm not into this sixties stuff. All you'll get for your trouble is dust in your face."

"Then why are you here?" Stefan already knew the answer to that. Zack had been sniffing after Carolina like a hound after a fox.

He shrugged. "Figured you could use some advice."

"We're doing just fine," Stefan said. "What we could use is a few more hands."

"Zack will help," Carolina said with a determined note in her voice. "Won't you, Zack?"

"For you?" he said, cocking his gun finger. "Sure."

A sign-up sheet was passed around, along with cups of lemonade and the chocolate chip cookies they'd made the night before. Then everybody took one of the signs and left. Everybody except Zack. Hank came out to get Stefan, and right as they were going into the house, Stefan heard Zack say, "How about going for a ride?"

He didn't hear Carolina's answer, but his heart stopped.

Stefan looked at Hank to see if he had heard, but Hank seemed to be listening only to the voices in his head these days.

Inside the house, Stefan waited for the longest time, straining his ears for the sound of Carolina's laughter or the gunning of a Harley engine, but all he could hear outside the screen door was the cooing of doves. Lovebirds, he figured. What else?

He knew that he could keep it from happening, keep her from riding off with Zack. All he had to do was tell Melanie, who wouldn't, for sure, let Carolina ride on the back of a Harley. Stefan chewed on the inside of his cheek. The truth was, it was none of his business. If Carolina wanted to go with Zack, he couldn't stop her. Well, he *could*, but then he'd never know if she would have gone of her own free will.

It was a warm night for Oregon. Stefan tried not to see it as a romantic kind of night, what with the moon and all, but he supposed it was. He picked up a *National Geographic* borrowed from the library and tried to look busy, but his ears were working overtime.

He heard them at last, two soft voices in the night, but he couldn't hear what they were saying, not a single word. He held his breath and listened as hard as he'd listened inside the forest, but it was no use. His ears were better tuned to hearing owls than girls. Then the Harley engine split the night in half and roared off. Stefan counted his heartbeats and tried to slow them to an idle.

"Great meeting, huh?" said Carolina, banging through the screen door. "Not too many people, but—"

"It was a great meeting!" Stefan cried, weak with relief. "*Great!* Oh, did Zack just leave?" He casually tossed the *National Geographic* onto the coffee table. "I thought I heard the Harley."

Carolina stuck her fists on her hips and frowned down at Stefan. "He's going to help, Stefan. We need all the hands we can get—you said so yourself. Why are you being so weird around him?"

"Right! Right! You're right," Stefan agreed, his spirits soaring because she hadn't gone with Zack. She had come back to be with him. Maybe she was losing patience, but what did that matter? She'd made a choice. She'd never pick a guy like Zack for a boyfriend.

What she didn't tell him was that Zack had agreed to carry a sign only if it was on her shift. Stefan didn't find that out until the next day, when Melanie asked if he was ready to go.

"Uh, sure," he said. "Where's Carolina?"

"She'll watch Trinity while we're gone," Melanie said. "The bird ladies will relieve us. Then Carolina and Zack will take the last shift."

Carolina and Zack!

"She's not riding with him, is she?" Stefan couldn't help himself, he had to know.

"Well, I said she could ride there and back. Only. And that she had to wear a helmet, of course."

"Good, Melanie," he said between clenched teeth. "That's great."

"Stefan?"

Stefan looked up and gave himself away, everything he'd been thinking and feeling.

"Oh," she said softly, biting her lip. "I didn't think about . . . I mean, I wasn't thinking. I'm sorry, Stefan."

"That's okay," he said, though his heart said it wasn't.

"I mean, it's not a date or anything. She's not allowed to date yet. And besides, he's . . . what? Sixteen? He's too old for her."

"Yeah, right."

"Oh, Stefan, you're jealous!" Her face was stuck in that crazy place between laughing and crying.

"Jealous, me? No way! I was just—just worried about her, that's all. Riding with . . . him." He shrugged, relieved to see Hank crossing the yard to help him into the back of the pickup.

"Oh, Stefan," Melanie crooned as if her heart would break. "Poor Stefan!"

16

MELANIE parked the pickup in the place they had chosen at the meeting, then lowered the tailgate. She got into the bed of the pickup and sat next to Stefan and the bag of snacks. "Well, here goes," she said, and held up her sign, the one that asked for honks. Stefan put up SAVE THE TREES, SAVE THE PLANET, and they waited for cars to pass.

Stefan hoped she wouldn't say anything more about Carolina and Zack. He hated having her feel sorry for him, as if he were some helpless little kid who couldn't take care of things himself. So he told her every joke he knew, the G-rated ones anyway, and tried to act as if everything was fine. Supercool. Or as his father said, "hunky-dory."

Some cars passed, not many. A few of them honked. Even though Stefan missed Carolina and wished she were there with him, it felt good to be at the forest again. Once he'd told Melanie all his jokes, he and she sat quietly side by side, letting the peacefulness of the place soak in.

It never felt to Stefan that they were alone. The trees looming overhead like friendly giants were so alive, he could almost hear them saying in tree language they were grateful somebody was there on guard.

He closed his eyes and listened to all the separate sounds the forest made. If he could hear tree language, he could probably hear bat wings, too, and the whirr of a flying squirrel as it leaped through the air, or the scurry of its claws in search of truffles. Spotted owls depended on a good supply of flying squirrels to survive. The truffle spores would be carried to other trees, where the fungus would help to water and nourish them. It had taken at least hundreds of years just to develop a certain rare ecosystem that couldn't be replaced ever again on the planet.

In his thirteen (so far) years there were some things he knew to be true. You had to protect the things that couldn't protect themselves. If you took care of the Earth, the Earth would take care of you. It was as simple (and as hard) as that.

"Melanie?"

"Hmmm?" Her eyes were closed, and Stefan noticed for the first time the dark circles under them. He guessed she was more worried than she let on.

"Couldn't Hank find some other kind of work besides cutting down trees? He says it's all he can do, but—"

She smiled a weary smile. "He feels terrible about all this, Stefan. He said not to tell you kids, but he didn't know this was a special kind of forest until he read some of those things you brought from the library. Trees have always been just trees to him. Lumber, like Dean said. Now he doesn't know what to do."

"Tell him I'm sorry, will you?"

He was beginning to feel like a sorry sap, apologizing to somebody every day for something.

"Sorry? What for, Stefan?"

"Well, for letting him down. He'll think I don't understand how hard this is for him, but I do."

"I'm sure he understands, Stefan."

But he had to tell her the rest, because he was just then figuring it out for himself. "You see, things have always been pretty easy for me."

Melanie gave Stefan a strange look. Easy? How could things ever be easy for a boy like Stefan?

"Well, sure, if I had a magic wish, I'd be a mountain climber or hike the John Muir Trail. I mean, who wouldn't? But my folks have lots of money, and I've been able to do whatever I wanted since I was a real little kid. Except leave home. Until now, I mean. I never wanted a whole lot, a lot of fancy *things*. I only wanted the chance to be a part of nature, to study nature, and I can."

Melanie smiled. She had a faraway look in her eyes, as if she could really see Stefan in the past, as a kid growing up.

"But here in Haskells Bay, here in the forest"—he looked up and took a deep, clean breath of air—"well, it isn't just reading about it or studying it from my window. It's, well, it's *real*. We could lose a whole ecosystem!"

Melanie sighed and shook her head.

"People can do other things to make a living. Hank can do something else. All the forest can do is—is grow. We can't let this thing happen, Melanie. We have to stop it. Somehow!"

And then Stefan was sure. There was only one right thing for him after all, if only he'd recognized it sooner.

She sighed again. "I know, honey."

"Two more days," he said miserably.

"Here comes another car," Melanie said. "Wave that sign, Stefan! We don't have much time."

One of Hank's logger buddies, a man named Willard, came screeching to a stop beside the pickup. "There's been an accident! Hank and Dean," he said, out of breath, as if he'd been running instead of driving.

Melanie jumped out of the truck. "What? Where? Is he all right? *Them*—are they all right? Where are they?"

Willard grabbed her arm to slow her down. "Dean's okay, scratches is all. Hank's on his way to Byron Memorial. That's all I know, honey. I'm sorry. Get in, I'll take you there."

"No, I . . . no. We'll drive, Stefan"—she turned her worried eyes on Stefan—"Stefan and I. Would you pick up Carolina and Trinity at the house, Willard? Bring them over? I mean, if it's bad—if Hank's—"

"Sure thing," said Willard. He whipped his big car around as fast as the highway patrol and raced for town.

"Oh, God," said Melanie. "Oh, Lord." She jumped into the cab, and they tore off toward Byron Memorial, the engine of Hank's old pickup clattering and whining at top speed. Stefan hung on in back while potato chips and cans of root beer went spilling everywhere. "Please let him be all right, please let him be all right," he said over and over again, until the words mashed together and didn't make sense anymore. It couldn't be true. How could anything happen to Hank? Hank was bigger than life. Nothing bad could happen to Hank!

They squealed into the hospital parking lot, and Melanie lurched to a stop. She jumped out, ran a few feet, and turned back around.

"It's okay," Stefan said, waving her on. "Go ahead."

"I'll send somebody out—"

"Go!" he said. She took off at a run.

Willard's car pulled up next to the pickup, and Carolina jumped out. "Oh, Stefan! This is so awful! Do you know what happened yet?"

Stefan said he didn't. He told her that Melanie was inside. Then he asked Willard if he could set up his chair and lift him out.

"That's one old-fashioned chair," Willard said, shaking his head. "Ain't seen one like that since, what? the Civil War?"

Dean was inside with Melanie, pacing the floor of the waiting room, scratching his head. "I don't know how it happened! Them brakes is new, brand-new. Hank and me are coming around the last turn before town, you know, right before the filling station, and . . . nothin'! I hit the brakes and *nothin'*! I couldn't believe it! And wouldn't you know, a church bus pulls out right in front of us. All's I could do was barrel over the side down into that old Christmas tree lot—"

"It's not your fault, Dean," Melanie said.

Willard clamped a hand on Dean's shoulder. "Why don't you go on over to the cafeteria, buddy? Get yourself a cup of coffee. Try and calm down. We'll tell you soon as we know something."

Dean looked at Willard as if Willard had told him to go shoot himself. "Right down to the floorboard," he said. "Stomped my foot right down to the floorboard. Wouldn't be surprised if I bent that brake pedal clean in half."

The waiting room was the kind of place you didn't want to hear bad news in. The lamps had dented, dusty shades, and the couches were made of orange plastic. Every last magazine had its cover torn off. Carolina sat in a shredded plaid chair, hugging her knees and rocking, looking faraway and frightened. Melanie couldn't stay seated. The minute she sat down, up she jumped again. "As long as he's alive," she said, "as long as he's alive."

At last a doctor came in. "Mrs. Macias?"

Melanie looked blank for a minute. She hadn't had that name all that long. "Yes?"

"Your husband's got some broken bones, right arm, left leg. How he managed that, I don't know. Anyway, he's going to be fine. We've got him sedated, but as soon as he's awake, you can see him."

"Oh, thank you!" cried Melanie, throwing her arms around the surprised doctor. "Thank you! You hear that, kids? He's all right. Hank's all right!"

Carolina jumped up and hugged her mom. Then Carolina grabbed and hugged Stefan, too. Her cheek was smooth and warm against his, and it hit him that they'd never hugged, never even held hands. Friends could do that, but they never did. "Oh, Stefan, isn't this the greatest thing? I mean, a broken arm and leg—that's bad, but it could have been so much worse!" She brushed a tear off her cheek.

Dean had collapsed into the chair that Carolina left. He'd put his face into his hands and was rocking his head back and forth. "Thank the Lord," he said several times, rocking and rocking his head as if he couldn't quite believe that Hank was alive.

They waited around until Hank woke up. Then they got to visit, two at a time. Melanie and Carolina went first. Hank was "grogged out," Carolina said, so they didn't stay long. "He's worried about how you're going to manage without him, Stefan. That's almost the first thing he said."

"Oh, no! What did you tell him?"

"I told him you hated taking showers anyway, that you wouldn't mind being a dirt ball for a while!"

"Thanks," Stefan said, without cracking a smile.

"Don't mention it."

On the way into Hank's room, Dean leaned over Stefan and said, "You need anything, my man, you let me know. Dean'll take care of ya." He looked embarrassed then, cleared his throat, and pushed open the door. "Hank, man!" he cried. "What the devil are you doing in here?"

Hank was white from the neck down. His left leg was wrapped and hanging in a sling, and his right arm, already in a cast, lay across his chest as if he'd be pledging the flag forever. " 'Lo, fellas," he said. His eyelids were at half mast.

"Hey, if you see the guy who decked me, knock him out with a two-by-four, would ya? He was too much for me!"

Dean laughed as if he'd heard the greatest joke in the world. Then he sobered up. "I don't know what happened, man," he said. "I can't figure it. Them brakes was just fixed." He threw up his hands and went into his story again.

"Hey, forget it, buddy," Hank said, cutting him off. "It's an old truck. Could have happened to anybody."

"Yeah," Dean muttered darkly, "but it didn't happen to just anybody. It happened to us. To you and me, man."

17

THE birder twins were the first to call. They'd heard about Hank's accident and offered to take Melanie's shift. They had discussed the situation at length, and they'd even talked about whether the protest should continue, considering what had happened. But if everybody else agreed, they said, the trees must still be fought for. As for them, they had decided that splitting up might be better after all. People would think one old lady was staying out there all day by herself, and they might feel guilty that they weren't doing anything. Or so the twins figured.

Melanie, Carolina, and Stefan had talked it over, too. It seemed wrong to carry on as if the accident hadn't happened. On the other hand, the six of them were all the trees had. All that stood between the trees and the chain saws.

They made a plan. Carolina and Stefan would baby-sit Trinity while Melanie was at the hospital, then Stefan would take care of Trinity by himself while Carolina and Zack did their shift.

Carolina and Zack.

He came for her right on time, hauling up the driveway on his Harley, scattering stones. Stefan gripped the arms of his chair and tried his best not to let his feelings show. It was all up to Carolina now, whatever happened between her and Zack. There was little—in fact, nothing—he could do.

Carolina grabbed her backpack. "You be good, Trinity," she said. "You do what Stefan tells you, okay?"

Trinity gave a solemn nod.

She looked at Stefan. "Are you sure you'll be all right?"

"What? You don't think she can take care of me?"

"You can always read *Goodnight Moon*. It knocks her right out."

"If it doesn't, I'll try boxing gloves. Or beer."

"Stefan!"

"Don't fall off that Harley," he warned. But of course the way not to fall off a motorcycle was to hold on tight to the guy in front, so no way could he win.

She ran off in a blaze of loose hair (why not the pony-tail?) and form-fitting jeans, four inches of bare back between a braided leather belt and her cut-off gray sweatshirt. Stefan held the screen door and watched until she was gone in a cloud of dust, waiting to see if she'd turn and wave. To let him know it was him she'd rather be with.

She didn't.

"Weed me a stowy," Trinity demanded.

"I'll weed you a billion stowies," he promised glumly. Anything to keep his overactive mind busy for the next three hours of Zack and Carolina's shift.

Two hours and forty-six minutes later he'd fed Trinity her dinner, played Chutes and Ladders (more or less), and read sixteen Golden Books and *Goodnight Moon* until he knew it by heart. At last Trinity nodded off.

Three hours.

Three hours and eighteen minutes. Stefan went to the front door, then the back, just to make sure they hadn't gotten past him somehow.

Three hours and twenty-three minutes.

At three hours and fifty-two minutes, he opened the refrigerator and ate the last piece of Melanie's two-week-old chocolate cake. Then he made a bologna sandwich and stuffed that down, too.

Stefan was furious, and then he was worried. Then he was furious all over again. He thought of all the things that could have happened between the house and Haskells Forest, in Haskells Forest. Zack wouldn't dare!

Would he?

Anyway, she wouldn't let him.

Would she?

He scooted his chair back and forth between the back door and the front door like a caged hamster. This time, he decided, he'd tell on her. He'd tell Melanie she didn't go straight to the protest point and back. If she didn't walk through that door in ten minutes . . . !

At four hours and five minutes, Stefan flipped off the light and sat in the dark. There was no place else for him to go. He could have waited in Carolina's room, but he had to watch that front door, had to catch the first glimpse of the Harley headlight as it came up the drive, no matter what.

Checking his watch up close to his face, Stefan refused to think the absolute worst—that they'd had an accident. Things didn't happen that way, one accident right after another. It was the law of averages.

So he thought about the second worst thing, that they were making out somewhere. Beyond that, his mind refused to go.

Like a bad song that sticks in your head and plays over and over like a weird kind of torture, he knew the sound of the Harley as it pulled up. Scooting to one side of the half-open door, he waited, his ears straining for any little sound once the engine died.

A laugh, soft. Hers.

His laugh then. Wicked-sounding, at least to Stefan's ears.

"Sure you could . . ." Zack said, and Stefan couldn't hear more. Could *what*?

She laughed again, a bell-like sound that only Carolina had. Stefan would have known that laugh in a crowded football stadium. Could have picked it right out.

They were closer to the door now. Stefan's heart was knocking hard, and his forehead was coated with sweat. He thought he could still make a run for it and be in his room when Carolina came in. But maybe not.

"Mmmmm," he heard Zack say.

"Hmmmm," Carolina said, and giggled.

Stefan could see them now, just a slice of them in the place where the open door was hinged to the frame. The full moon made a hazy outline around their two tall shapes, without a sliver of light between. Stefan saw Zack's head lean down, saw Carolina's chin go up. And then, while his heart cried *no, please, no,* he watched Carolina get kissed.

A sweet kiss. For Zack. For what Stefan would have expected of Zack. He just leaned down and touched her lips for a minute, maybe less. It seemed a whole lot longer to Stefan, watching, an agony of time. But then he wasn't the one doing it.

That was what came of not taking care of business, Dean would have said. But what could he have done? In the movies the hero would have grabbed the girl long before this and dragged her off to his cave or whatever. But in the movies the hero never rode into town in a wheelchair.

When Zack took his face away from Carolina's, hers stayed where it was. As if she'd been shocked. Electrocuted.

And then she was standing by herself, Carolina in the fuzzy moonlight. And Stefan heard the Harley roar off.

"Sorry I'm late." Her voice was high and fluttery as she came through the door. "Zack took me over to see Hank. I called you a couple of times, but the phone was busy. Did your mother call or something?" She went over to the telephone. With a chuckle, she put the receiver back into its cradle. "Trinity does this all the time. I should have warned you. Everything all right?"

"Huh? Oh, yeah. It's fine. Everything all right with you?"

She gave Stefan a strange look. "Yeah, sure. Why?"

"I dunno," said Stefan with an exaggerated shrug. "Just checkin'. Well, good night," he said, and spun around to go back into the bedroom. How could he sit there another minute without telling her what he had seen, without asking her how she could kiss that creep? That L.A. creeped-out biker! And how many other boys had she kissed? Even though he sort of knew that Zack had been the first. She still looked stung, as if she'd come back from a place very far away, an exciting, dangerous place she'd had the tiniest peek at.

"Stefan?"

He turned at the door to her room.

"Don't you want to wait for Melanie?"

"Huh?"

"Well"—she shrugged—"Hank's not here to help you get into bed."

"Oh," he said, feeling like an idiot. "Right. I guess I wasn't thinking."

"So do you want to play Scrabble or something? I mean, until Mom gets home?"

He shrugged. "I guess," he said over the lump that had formed in his throat.

She took out the board and set it up. They each drew their seven letters, then an extra tile to see who would go first.

"Okay," said Carolina, "you go. I don't have anything good anyway." She put her elbows on the table and rested her chin in the cup of her hands.

Stefan tried not to stare at her, but it was hard for him

not to. She looked the same as always, the tiny mole under her eye, the eighteen freckles on her nose. Still, every time he looked up from the letters he was trying to make a word with, he was surprised to see the same Carolina. In the space of a few minutes, less than that, his whole world had crashed, and there she was, just the same.

Could a girl get kissed and act like nothing happened? Was she pretending just for him?

Maybe it *didn't* matter. Maybe she'd forgotten all about it already, while he sat there driving himself crazy.

Who was he kidding? It mattered. There was no way a kiss *couldn't* matter. She was thinking about it all right. A kiss from a boy would matter all right. He knew Carolina well enough to know that.

But who was he, Stefan Crouch? Carolina's friend, sure. A friend of nature, he'd always been that. But beyond those things, who was he? Who was the flesh-and-blood Stefan? He wasn't stupid; he knew the way nature worked, the birds and bees stuff, long before most other kids. It didn't embarrass him or make him giggle; mating was simply the way things worked. At his school, where boys and girls were already pairing up, he told himself it didn't matter that the girls didn't see him as a real guy. But it mattered. It mattered that he'd wanted to kiss Carolina from the minute he saw her in the airport, and that he hadn't done it first. It would always matter.

He shuffled the letters on his rack, but they kept turning up the same word: LOVE. He'd give up his turn before he made that one. REVOL, he made, wishing he had a "T" instead of a stupid "C." He shuffled the letters again and made LOVER. He was about to give up when the "C" showed itself to be a friend after all. CLOVER he laid across the middle of the board.

Carolina frowned. "You're too lucky," she said. "You win every game we play!"

"Yeah," Stefan sighed. "I'm one lucky guy."

≫

Later, after Melanie and Carolina had gotten Stefan into bed, Carolina came running back. "Stefan!" she cried. "The brake lines were cut!"

18

By the next morning, the whole town was buzzing with the news. The telephone rang every ten minutes. Finally Melanie just gave up and sat by it, waiting for the next ring.

"Is it true?"

"You tell Hank we'll get to the bottom of this!"

"Can you believe this could happen in Haskells Bay?"

Dean came by that afternoon with the latest word. "It was Otto," he said, "that old SOB. Friend of mine over at the sheriff's office says they're goin' down to arrest him. They're probably on their way right now."

"Otto?" Carolina cried. "No way! He wouldn't do something like that!"

"You heard him at the town meeting, Carolina," Dean said. "You heard him plain as day, making them death threats."

"He said that to Mr. Farnsworth, not you, not Hank! And besides, Otto's all talk. He doesn't mean half the things he says. Come on, Stefan!"

They headed for the bay, nearly toppling over tree roots and the splintered boards of the dock on their way, and got there right behind the sheriff. His black-and-white car was parked with its motor running, its red light slowly spinning. Carolina and Stefan watched as two officers pinned Otto's arms behind him and took out the handcuffs.

"Not on my boat," growled Otto, looking like they'd pulled him straight out of bed. The collar of his red flannel PJs stuck up from under his fisherman's sweater. He straightened his shoulders as best he could. "I am the captain on this boat!"

The officers looked over Otto's head at each other. Then, almost gently, they escorted Otto off the *Hannah Marie* and cuffed him on the dock. Stefan found it hard to believe that the old man could have done what they said, but the police believed otherwise.

"I didn't do it," he said as they passed. "You kids know I wouldn't do something like that."

"We know, Otto," Carolina said at once, but Stefan wasn't so sure. Otto's anger was never far beneath the surface. It could erupt in seconds and send you flying from the deck with nothing but a thirteen-year-old girl's determination to save you. The whiskey, which was never out of reach, gave him false courage.

They watched the officers stow Otto in the back of their car and drive off, light still spinning but no siren, as if there were no real hurry.

"Poor Otto!" Carolina said. "Don't they have to prove he did it? Find the weapon or something?"

"A good sharp fishing knife would do it," Stefan said.

"Oh, Stefan, you don't really believe that."

He shrugged. "Maybe not. I can't really picture him climbing under a truck and all that. He's more the impulsive type. But who, then?"

They had been making their way up the path when Carolina suddenly stopped. Stefan turned and saw that Carolina's face had gone chalk-white. "What's wrong?"

"Do you remember when we were talking about, you know, riots and stuff . . ."

"Zack?"

The color flooded back into her face, and she tried to laugh off whatever she was thinking. "No, that's crazy. I don't know what made me think—"

But Stefan jumped right on it. "You're right!" he said. "He told you about putting sugar in gas tanks and stuff!"

"Yeah, but not—not about cutting brake lines. Not really dangerous things like that!"

"Still!"

"He wouldn't do that. He wouldn't try to kill somebody!"

"Why not? He said you had to do something more than a peaceful protest." Stefan moved in for the kill. "And remember how he spun out of the parking lot the first time we ever saw him? He's got his grandfather's hot temper. He could have done it, Carolina!"

"I'm sorry I ever said anything," she said tightly. "Now you're building this—this case! Like you're a detective or something."

"But you're the one who thought—"

"Forget it, Stefan! Forget I ever said anything. Zack wouldn't do a thing like that."

"He went after Dean at the wedding! I saw him!"

"When? You're making that up!" Carolina pushed Stefan's chair furiously up the hill.

"Why would I make up a thing like that?"

"Because you don't like Zack, that's why!" Carolina said hotly. She stopped pushing at the base of the ramp, out of breath. Palms on her thighs, she leaned over, filling her lungs.

"Well, *you* do," said Stefan, before he could stop himself, "so that makes one of us."

Carolina stared at Stefan wide-eyed. "So?"

"So you do!" he said. "You *do* like him!"

"Well." She shrugged, scuffing the toe of her sneaker into the dirt. Her thumbs were hooked into the pockets of her jeans. "Sure. I guess. I mean, why shouldn't I?" She looked up, challenging Stefan with that same little lift of her chin.

"No reason," Stefan said miserably.

"He's just a friend," she insisted.

"Yeah," said Stefan, "I know. Like you and me, right? Friends."

She frowned. "No, not like you and me—different."

He swallowed hard. "How?"

"Huh?"

"How different?"

She threw up her hands. "I don't know, Stefan! Just *different*!" She pushed him up the ramp.

"Guess what, kids?" Melanie said with a big smile, as Stefan and Carolina came into the house. "Dean's bringing Hank home this afternoon!"

"Great!" said Carolina.

"Great!" said Stefan.

Melanie caught something in their voices. "Are you guys all right? Did you hear what I said? Hank's coming home! And guess what? Our protest made the news. We're bound to have a crowd now!"

"Hey, Bud," Hank said to Stefan as he came motoring up the ramp in his rented wheelchair. "I guess I made this thing for myself after all!" Hank was in a great mood, which came from having things not be worse than they were. He could have landed on his head, Melanie said, instead of his leg and arm, but Hank laughed and said that all he'd have gotten from that would have been a headache, hard as his head was. "Now what you need to getcha, Stefan," he said, patting the arm of his rented chair, "is one of these. See? You just push a button, and you go into superwarp!" Hank was talking more than they'd ever heard him. He even told a couple of corny doctor jokes he'd picked up at the hospital. But he fell asleep at the dinner table, his bearded chin nestled on his chest.

Dean stayed the night, sleeping on the couch. Hank and Stefan were lucky to have him, but work would start tomorrow for Dean. Tomorrow, unless a miracle happened, they'd cut the first big trees in Haskells Forest.

After dinner Carolina washed the dishes, and Stefan dried

them. Neither said a word until the very last glass. Then Stefan went for broke. All she could do was say no.

"Let's go to the forest," he said, "one more time. Before it's, well, in case it's . . ."

Carolina rinsed a glass and passed it over to Stefan. She frowned, thinking. "It's late," she said at last. He could tell she wanted to be friends again, to forget the things they'd said in anger.

"Don't you want to see the forest at night?"

"Well, sure, but I don't think Melanie will take us this late."

"No, just us," he insisted. "You and me. Besides, Melanie has to stay here with Trinity. Hank can't watch her." They were whispering now.

"But how can we get there?"

"Walk," he said. "I mean, if you can walk it, I can roll. It's not that far."

"Melanie will never let us."

Their eyes met. "Remember when we used to sneak out of my house?" Stefan said. "Remember how much fun it was?"

"We were just kids," Carolina said, but she smiled for the first time all evening, remembering.

"It was fun," he insisted.

"Yeah," she agreed, "it was."

"Well?"

"I'll come and get you when I know they're asleep," she said.

"Cool," he said.

Stefan dried the last plate and handed it to Carolina to put away. "It's time for another adventure, right?"

"It's time to say goodbye," she said sadly.

Stefan's heart nearly stopped, for good and ever. "To the trees, you mean."

"Yeah," she said, "to the trees."

❧

Afterward Stefan thought it was funny that Melanie went off to her room without offering to help him into bed. Did she guess what he and Carolina were up to? If she did, she understood the way only Melanie could how much he would need to go one last time to the forest. Something had planted itself like a seedling in his mind, starting the night Carolina first pushed him up the hill and the dark thing had settled in. He needed to think about what would come next and what he would do. He needed to be inside those trees and listen to them one more time. And he needed Carolina beside him. If he could think of something, some miraculous thing, everything would be perfect again. The trees, him, and Carolina. Everything.

❧

She came for him when the house and all that lay around it were still. The night seemed to be humming, waiting to escort them on their way.

They went as quietly as they could down the loose stones of the drive, Grandpa being extra quiet as if the man himself were helping them make their escape. It was Stefan's grandfather who had found the land the Crouches still lived on and bought it because of its hundreds of trees. Stefan knew Grandpa would have understood. He hoped an old man's wisdom would seep into him somehow, that he would think of something to save the trees before it was too late.

They started off along the road, shining their flashlights in two yellow beams, ducking out of sight the second they heard a car. If anybody saw them out so late—two kids, one in a wheelchair, heading down the main road—they'd have stopped for sure. Or at least called the sheriff from their cell phone.

Stefan's arms were feeling strong as pistons as he whipped Grandpa through his paces. Carolina's long legs took the road at an easy stride.

Perhaps because they'd been too busy before, or because the night was right for memories, they began to reminisce about all the things they had done when they were eleven, when they had first met and when Carolina had Crow.

"I still miss him," she said. "I miss him all the time. He was my best friend—besides you, I mean. I never say that to anybody else, though. Nobody understands how a bird can be your best friend."

"I was thinking maybe we should have marked him somehow," Stefan said. "Then I'd know for sure if I saw him. We could have put a band on his leg or something."

"No," she said quickly. "When I let him go, I wanted to let him all-the-way go. It wouldn't have been right to hold him back, not even with a band. He'd always know one part of him wasn't free, was still attached to somebody besides himself."

"Yeah."

"It's like us, kinda," she said.

"Like us?" Stefan's stomach did a cartwheel.

"Well, yeah, a little." Stefan could tell she'd been thinking about the words they'd had coming up the hill from the dock. So had he. "No matter what, we'll always be together. Even when we're not. We don't need anything to remind us that we're best friends. Right?"

"Right," he said, and thought about the little silver ring stuffed deep into a pocket of his suitcase.

"Real friends don't need reminders," she said.

❧

It was superdark where the trees began and made their tunnel over the road. Too dark to see, until their eyes grew used to it. "Are you scared?" Carolina said.

Stefan wanted to say no, because he was the guy, and because it had all been his idea to begin with. But except for the fib about the pearl earrings, he'd never told Carolina anything but the truth. "A little," he said.

"There are bears, you know."

"I know."

"We should have brought a baseball bat or something!"

"The trees will protect us," Stefan said. He knew he sounded crazy, but he said it anyway, because it was truly what he believed right then. It was like drawing a magic chalk circle and then stepping inside it. He knew somehow they'd be all right once they were in the forest.

After some searching with their flashlights, they found

the place that had opened up for them before. Only this time they went deeper in, using their lights to guide them around decaying logs and broken branches. Trees loomed up on all sides, silent as soldiers on sentry duty.

"Whoa!" said Stefan. His light had caught two glittering eyes, but he blinked and they were gone.

"What was it?"

"A possum, probably," he whispered. But he'd never heard of a four-foot possum, and that was about where the eyes had been. If they really were eyes.

They came to a small natural clearing, a place where they were surrounded by some of the very tallest trees. "If we're very quiet," Stefan said, "maybe we'll hear the spotted owls."

They turned off their flashlights, and Carolina sat beside Stefan's chair on a log. They listened and waited, breathing together their careful quiet breaths. The forest sounds came up around them like an orchestra starting, all on different notes and in different keys, tuning up. And then they could actually hear a kind of rhythm in it, in the clicking of beetles, the scurry of chipmunks, the dripping of water from the leaves. Stefan reached for Carolina's hand, full of a kind of confidence, or foolishness, that said it didn't matter if she took it or not. But of course it did. She looked up at Stefan. In the dark he could barely make out the smile that crossed her face, but it was there all right. She took a firm hold of his hand, and that's how they were sitting when they heard the first owl.

"Hoo . . . hoo-hoo . . . hooo!"

Carolina's breath caught. She and Stefan squeezed hands.

"Hoo-hoo!" came a return cry. Then a swoop of wings very near.

"Are they spotted owls?" Carolina whispered.

"Sure," Stefan said confidently, though he wasn't sure at all.

"Oh, Stefan!" said Carolina. "I'll never forget this! I'll never forget we heard a real spotted owl!"

As they sat, still holding hands, Stefan tried as hard as he could to listen to the trees. Even if they couldn't actually talk, he figured they'd try to send some kind of nonverbal message. Like captives in some hostile territory who could communicate only with their eyes or tap Morse code on a rock, they'd try to tell him what to do to save them. But if they were trying, he wasn't getting it. It was going to be all up to him after all. Which was how, he'd learned, things usually were anyway.

After a while they made their way back home. As they headed down the dark road, Stefan could feel the trees fading behind him, and he turned once in a panic to make sure they were still there.

But he knew it was all over. What could a kid like him do against a tree killer like Coastal Lumber?

19

IN the morning they got up extra early. Dean said the trucks would be moving in at eight. Melanie hugged Hank, then headed with Trinity out the door. Stefan waited for Carolina, who'd gone out to put all the signs in the truck.

"Bud?" Hank said. "You be careful."

It surprised Stefan, how serious Hank's face was. "Me?"

"Be careful, hear?" With a little nod to show he meant business.

Stefan stopped mid-roll. Always Melanie was the one who reminded them to be careful. The warning was kind of spooky, coming from Hank. Almost as if Hank knew something that Stefan didn't know, something about him and what he might do. But Stefan said he'd be careful. He was sure then that he would be.

❧

About the time they should have gotten to the protest point, Stefan felt the pickup slow down. Carolina popped up to see what was going on. "There's somebody there," she said. "A whole bunch of people!"

"Hurrah!"

"Stefan, it's the TV!"

"Huh?"

"One of those TV trucks, with the thing, the dish, on the top!"

Half the town had gathered at the forest. Getting into the spirit of things—and hoping they might get on TV—a few people had made signs and were marching back and forth across the road and singing "Trees shall overco-o-ome, trees shall overco-o-ome!" But most of the people were laughing and joking, as if they'd come to a big party. Carolina glowered at them. It wasn't a party; it was serious business.

Stefan scanned the crowd for Zack. It would be just like him not to show on the most important day of all.

Then right when he thought the water was free of sharks, up the road came the big black Harley. Spotting the truck, Zack skidded alongside and stopped, wearing the same black jacket he had had on the night they first saw him. A duffel bag was strapped onto the backseat. "Sorry I can't hang out with you all," he said.

Carolina froze. "Where are you going?"

"Gotta get back to L.A." He shrugged. "My ma's sick." He shook his hair back.

"Oh, I'm sorry," said Carolina at once. "Is it bad?"

"Yeah," Zack said dramatically. "Something to do with her—her appendix, or something."

"Won't they just take it out?"

"Well, sure! Sure they will. But it's not only that."

"Oh," said Carolina, but she knew better than to push him. "Well, I'm sorry you have to go. I mean, your grandfather probably needs you right now."

"Oh, he's not in jail anymore. They released him on bail. Until the trial."

Carolina smoothed a finger over the shiny chrome handlebar. "You don't think he really did it, do you, Zack?"

"Nah," said Zack, sticking out his right boot and squinting at the toe as if he might learn something there. "Otto's too smashed at night to get himself off the boat. He didn't do it."

"Were you with him that night, Zack?" she asked softly.

"Hey, what's with all these questions? You sound like the FBI."

Carolina blushed and looked down. "I thought maybe you could be his, you know, alibi."

He frowned and looked away. "Well, I wasn't on the boat that night, so I can't help him."

"Maybe not," Carolina said quietly. "Well, I hope your mom gets better."

"Huh? Oh, yeah! Take it easy, pretty girl," he said, and gave her his two-fingered salute. Gunning the engine, he roared off, helmetless, the wings of his black hair flying.

Carolina plunked down on the tailgate, her legs kicking back and forth. Her head was down, and whatever she was thinking drew a frown across her forehead. Stefan waited.

"I did a bad thing," she said finally.

"You?" he said, trying to make light of whatever it was. Carolina had never done a really bad thing in her life.

"Zack *did* talk about brake lines," she said. "When he told me about the riots. I tried to pretend I was making it up, that I didn't really hear him say that. But I did. And now he's gone! He's going to get away with it." Stefan had never seen her so miserable.

"You need to tell the sheriff," he said. "They can catch up with him."

"Why did I do such a dumb thing, Stefan?" she asked, tears in her eyes.

Stefan tried to answer but ended up shrugging instead. How could he tell her if she really didn't know?

❧

Ten till eight, and a TV announcer was making her way through the crowd, asking people for their opinions. Everybody wanted a chance to be on camera, but only a few people could come up with a single good reason why the forest shouldn't be cut down.

"I dunno," said one young mother with a baby in a backpack. "I guess we got enough paper in the world already. I mean, we have to recycle *everything* these days!"

"Well, there won't be shade here anymore," said a kid about Stefan and Carolina's age, looking up as if he were seeing the trees for the first time.

The announcer threaded her way through the crowd. "Over here!" Carolina said, pointing at Stefan. "Ask him!"

Stefan was ready this time. He cleared his throat, held

the mike steady, and began: "Some of these trees are over eight hundred years old," he said. "There are birds and all kinds of animals that will lose their homes, that will even go extinct if—"

"Thank you," said the announcer, snatching back the mike and whipping on to somebody else. She was looking for a sound bite, not an ecology lecture. Carolina gave Stefan a high five. He'd had his say at last, or anyway he'd tried to.

Carolina was getting more and more upset that nobody was taking the protest seriously. When she couldn't stand it any longer, she leaped onto the back of the pickup, waved her arms, and yelled for attention. A half-dozen people turned to see what all the commotion was. "Hey, you guys!" she yelled. "This isn't a party, you know! When the trucks come up this road"—she pointed her long arm—"they'll be coming to cut down the forest, our forest. It's not too late to stop them! It's not too late to save Haskells Forest!"

About three people clapped.

Carolina jumped down. "They don't believe it's really going to happen, do they?"

"I guess not," Stefan said, glumly. They wandered along the road up to the front so that they could be the first to spot the trucks when they came. But the birder twins were already there, in their matching tweed jackets and identical frowns, holding up their signs. "Save the trees!" they chanted. "Save the trees!" Carolina and Stefan chanted with them, trying to get people to join in.

The sheriff's car came slowly up the road. It parked, and the deputies stayed inside, keeping an eye on things.

Stefan looked at Carolina. She sighed and looked away. Then, still frowning but determined, she crossed the road over to the black-and-white car. Stefan saw her point down the road. When she came away, a single whoop went up, and the red light spun. People got out of the way, and the sheriff's car sped off, south, the way Zack had gone.

"I told them," Carolina said when she'd come back to him. "I told them about Zack."

"Good," said Stefan, feeling much better than he had a right to feel.

"Am I a rat?"

"Yup!" He grinned.

"*Stefan!*"

"You did the right thing, Carolina," he said seriously. "You did the right thing."

"I know," she said, her eyes welling with tears, "but it hurts just the same."

❧

They heard the big engines before they saw them, coming from a long way off, like an army on the move. "They're here!" Carolina cried. People began moving to the sides of the road, pulling back their children, peering expectantly in the direction of the gathering roar.

"Hank!" Trinity cried, plain as day, pointing her baby finger at the first truck as it appeared in the distant haze.

"That's not Hank, Trinity," Carolina said grimly. "That's the bad guys, coming to get the trees."

"Oh, Lord, this is terrible!" cried Melanie.

The trucks looked like giant bulldogs, with flat chrome

snouts. Sunlight glinted off the first snout a football field away, below the rise that would bring them up to the trees. There were three trucks in all, the roar of their combined engines so loud Stefan and Carolina had to yell to be heard. COASTAL LUMBER said the writing on their doors, in happy yellow letters. The dark green trucks looked brand-new, or else they'd been washed and waxed for this special day. Stefan wondered which truck Dean was in. Could he see them waiting there?

"Save the trees!" cried the birder twins. "Save the trees!" Two lonely voices that refused to give up.

Then Stefan began to get nervous. Why weren't the trucks slowing down? The first driver could see the people on both sides of the road, but he came straight on. It was kind of spooky, half a field away now and climbing. Gears changed, and the pitch of the engines rose. Stefan turned to look at the trees, at the people who were such a thin barrier between them and the trucks, and not even that. Everybody had gone quiet, watching the trucks come on as if waiting for the start of a parade, or maybe a funeral procession. They were well off the road, even the few who were carrying signs.

The first truck loomed into full view over the rise, heat rising in waves from its hood, and before he even knew exactly what he was doing, Stefan slapped Grandpa's wheels into motion. Behind him he heard voices, a few, then more: "What's he doing?" "Hey, kid!" "Somebody stop that kid!" Then Carolina and Melanie together, "Stefan!" their voices panicky and high. But Stefan kept on going. He fixed his eyes on the shiny chrome snout of the first truck and, with every cell in his body, willed it to stop. But it kept right on coming, the snout looming larger, the smell of diesel fuel thick in the air. Things slowed down then, as if they were all caught in some strange kind of dream together, the people, him, the trees. He saw Dean's face high in the cab of the first truck, his one good eye wide. He watched the passenger door open, slowly, slowly. Dean swung halfway out. "Stefan, what the hell?" His voice came out of a deep tunnel. "S-t-e-f-a-n!"

Brakes screeched, and the first truck skidded to a stop, smoke rising up from the tires, surrounding Grandpa and Stefan in a thick gray cloud. Stefan could have reached out and poked the truck right in the snout, but his hands were shaking so badly he had to hold real tight to Grandpa. Dean came tearing around the truck. "What are you doing, buddy? You coulda been killed!"

Then everybody was everywhere, a sea of faces and voices all around him. Carolina wriggled her way through. "Stefan! Stefan, I was so scared! I couldn't move! Why did you do that?"

But she didn't really expect him to answer, and he couldn't have anyway. When the people cleared away, and the smoke, there were three monstrous trucks in a line, and all their engines were silent.

"Tammy Broadbent, Channel Five News," said a skinny lady in a bright red suit and dyed yellow hair. "This young man"—she stuck her mike in Stefan's face—"what's your name, young man?"

"His name is Stefan Millington Crouch," pronounced

Carolina in a clear, loud voice. "Stefan Millington Crouch the Third."

"Stefan Millington Crutch," said the announcer into the camera, "has done a remarkable thing. Some would call it foolish, but this boy has just faced down thousands of pounds of solid steel. He has put his life on the line and virtually brought this operation to a halt." She stuck the mike in Stefan's face again. "Tell our viewers what made you—"

Stefan spun Grandpa and headed, fast as he could go, in the direction of the trees. He'd had enough of people.

Behind him he could hear Carolina saying all the things he should have said, now that he had his chance, but she was saying them for him as well as for herself. And for the trees, most of all for the trees.

20

IT was all over the news. ABC, NBC, CNN, *Time* and *Newsweek, Mother Jones.* Even *The Wall Street Journal,* his father's favorite newspaper.

Stefan thought his mother would have a heart attack at first, but then she was on the telephone all day long bragging, though she tried to make it sound like something else.

"Our *crazy* son! Yes, that's really him on the cover of *Newsweek* in that old relic of a wheelchair staring straight up at that enormous truck! I thought I'd *die,* of course. Well, he has very strong beliefs, you know. Just like his father."

Stefan wasn't home ten minutes before his father sat him down for one of his lectures—well, his father sat down. But for once his father said nothing. They both knew that what Stefan had done was foolish, no need to say it. Stefan had already thought of everything his father could have said and more. But he'd do it again if he had to.

His father finally shook his head and patted Stefan's knee. "We're glad you're home safe, son. That's what matters."

But it wasn't all that mattered.

The trucks left that day, after first putting in a call to the boss. Mr. Farnsworth was concerned about the image of Coastal Lumber. He wasn't in any great hurry to start cutting down the trees after all. The media were hounding him. In the meantime, Carolina told Stefan on the phone, a Sierra Club attorney had filed for an injunction. That could tie things up at least for a while. But since Haskells Forest was private property, maybe nothing at all could be done, and the trucks would be back, this time to stay.

Zack was arrested that afternoon and brought back to Haskells Bay, where he finally admitted to cutting the brake lines and nearly causing the death of two loggers. When they asked him why he had done it, he didn't seem to have a good answer. It wasn't to save the trees apparently; he just didn't like loggers. He didn't like the way they looked at him. Attempted murder, the district attorney said. But since Zack was a minor, he wouldn't be going to jail. He'd do his time in a juvenile detention facility. The prince had become a common frog, after all, and not even a very nice frog.

Carolina was fishing with Otto again, but they needed their best winch man, she said.

❧

The night before he left Haskells Bay, Stefan did what he'd absolutely decided not to do: He gave Carolina the ring. He knew it was stupid after what she'd said about the two of them not needing anything to remind them they were friends, but by then he was getting used to doing stupid things and thinking about them later.

Stefan's plane was scheduled to leave at seven the next morning, and it was a long ride to the airport. He was already packed. Carolina had put Trinity to bed, and she, Hank, and Stefan were playing gin rummy, waiting for Melanie to come home. In she came with a big smile and the fixings for root beer floats.

"Now I know a little about how your mother felt having Carolina stay with y'all," she said. "I feel like you're family, Stefan. It's like you've always been in our lives, you know?"

Stefan looked at Carolina, whose eyes were shining and sad. "I know," he said, his voice cracking.

They had their floats, and then Melanie gave a big fake yawn and said she was sleepy. "Aren't you, Hank?"

"Well, no, not—" Then he caught on. "Oh, yeah. Guess I am. Must be all this wheeling around!"

Then Stefan and Carolina had the room to themselves. But the dock was where they both wanted to be.

~

They were quiet as they set off down through the trees for the last time. Stefan was figuring they'd finally run out of things to say, exactly what had worried him most on the flight up the coast. But they weren't out of words, they were each in that place you have to go before you say goodbye.

Carolina pushed Grandpa, although she didn't have to,

never had to, and Stefan watched the moon cast the tall shadows of pines and firs up over his legs. Down the road, the trees of Haskells Forest had lived another day, a single day. But it was a victory.

They rattled to the end of the dock, and Carolina set the brake. She sat down on the rough boards and laid her head against Stefan's knees. Together they looked out across the dark water. Ghost clouds floated in front of the moon and a handful of twinkling stars.

"Maybe your folks could buy a vacation house up here," Carolina said.

Stefan knew he wouldn't be talking his parents into anything for a good long time.

"I don't want to wait another two years to see you again," she said. "It's not fair that we should be this many miles apart."

"I brought you another present," Stefan said, and heard the way the words came right out, as if someone else were responsible for saying them.

She turned her face to look up at him.

"But you can't have it unless you promise not to give it back, no matter what." He knew it wasn't fair, but he wasn't thinking fair right then. He was on a roll, the kind where your mouth goes tumbling forward, faster than your mind.

"Why would I give it back?"

"Because . . . because . . ." He shrugged. "I dunno. Because maybe you wouldn't want it."

"Well, what is it?"

"Guess," he said, feeling like a six-year-old.

"Is it bigger than a breadbox?"

"Nope."

"Smaller than a mouse?"

"Yup."

She was quiet for a minute. Stefan panicked, thinking she'd guessed what it was.

"I don't have anything for you," she said. "And you already gave me that great picture of Crow. I don't think I want another present right now."

"You don't?"

"Nope."

The air came out of him in a rush. "Huh," he said, like a caveman.

"Maybe you could keep it, like, for my birthday or something."

"I suppose I could."

"Stefan?"

"Huh?"

"Nothing."

"Don't *do* that!"

"Don't be mad, okay?" She turned her face, the face he loved most in the whole world, and he bit harder on his lip to hold back his tears. She didn't want it. She knew it was a ring, and she didn't want it.

"I'm not mad, Carolina."

"Okay, then," she said, and her forehead went smooth

again. "Good. And if you see Crow, call me right away, okay? I mean, right that minute."

"You know I will."

"And if he gives you, like, a message or anything—well, just listen real hard, okay? You don't think it's dumb, do you?"

"Of course not."

"Stefan?"

"Is this a trick?"

"Nope."

"Okay, then what?"

"Zack wasn't, you know, anything special." She shrugged. "I mean, in case you thought he was."

The ring was burning a hole in his mind. "You don't have to keep this if you don't want to," he said, pulling out of his pocket the little silver dolphin. "You won't hurt my feelings. It's just a friendship thing." He held it out on the palm of his hand, thinking because a ring could be both beautiful and strong, how perfect it was for Carolina.

She said nothing for about three years, or so it felt to him. She stared at the little silver circle that the dolphin made, nose to tail. "Oh, Stefan," she said in a voice he couldn't read. "It's so beautiful." And then she reached up and plucked it off his palm.

He watched her hold up her right hand and slip the little ring over her fourth finger, and when it wouldn't go, over her pinkie. "It's just right," she said.

"I know you said we didn't need, like, *things* to—"

"It's just right, Stefan," she said, and again, more softly but with the same sureness in her voice, "it's just right."

❧

There are these little pieces of time when all the world is right. When everyone you know is safe, when birds fly free, and when trees go on breathing as if no end will ever come to them. When you wouldn't be anybody else, no matter how handsome, or lucky, or perfectly made. For Stefan, that night on the dock with Carolina was one of those times.

This, too, was the truth as far as he knew it: Love was everywhere. It wasn't always exactly what you asked for, or maybe when you asked for it. It came in its own good time and in its own way, and it didn't always have a name to call it by. It was a fragile thing, like a bird perched for a second on your shoulder, or a seed sprouting a new tree. You had to hold on to it, but only in your heart. Even after it was gone.